Escape from Behruz

by

Judy Meadows

Escape from Behruz

Cover Art by *Diana Carlile*

The Wild Rose Press, Inc.
PO Box 708
Adams Basin, NY 14410-0708
Visit us at www.thewildrosepress.com

Publishing History
First Champagne Rose Edition, 2017
Print ISBN 978-1-5092-1403-7
Digital ISBN 978-1-5092-1404-4

Published in the United States of America

"What do you want?"

He could scarcely remember his reason for coming to her room. It had been overridden by an overwhelming urge to touch her. Her feminine softness pulled at every cell in his body. "I've brought your puppy. Can I come in for a minute?"

"Oh." Her eyes shifted uneasily to the empty hallway and then to the corner of the room, to something out of Rashid's sight. "I don't think it's a good idea. I was getting ready for dinner. I…"

She seemed almost too flustered to speak. Why? He wanted to grab her, use force, do anything he had to do to get her out of Behruz, but there would be no sneaking across the border with an unwilling hostage, especially if the border officials had been put on the alert to watch for that hostage.

"I'm sorry, Livie. I need to talk to you. Let me come in for a few minutes, and then we can go down to dinner."

"All right." She let him push his way past her into the room and close the door. "Let me see the puppy first." She reached to take him from Rashid's arm.

"No. I don't think… Your dress—"

"Never mind the stupid dress!" She reached for the puppy. She was shaking. He felt the tremor on his arm when she slid her hand under the puppy.

There was a little thud behind Rashid. Olivia's eyes darted from the puppy to the source of the sound and then to Rashid.

What? He swung around. A baby boy was using the bedpost to pull himself up from the floor.

Olivia went stony still and pale.

Chapter One

Rashid was coming back.

She wouldn't see him, of course. Abu-Khan would make sure of that.

But he was coming.

Olivia pulled back the heavy silk curtain that framed the only window in the room. A sliver of anticipation sliced through her. Maybe she *would* see him.

She gazed down at the lush expanse of lawn and the high stone wall beyond. There were soldiers, more than usual, milling around the guard station by the main entrance to the palace. One of the officers must have barked some command, because the soldiers suddenly formed a line and snapped to attention. They began maneuvering their rifles from side to side in a drill she'd seen many times before.

Why were there so many soldiers? What was going on?

A soft tapping interrupted her musing, and she went to the door. It was Jamal's young nanny, Nargess, with Jamal on her hip.

"Good morning, *khanoum*." The girl pronounced the title of respect for women in the guttural Farsi of her village near the Iranian border. "Do you want me to put Jamal down for his nap?"

"No, I'll do it. Thank you." Olivia took the sleepy

toddler in her arms and settled his head into the hollow between her shoulder and her neck. She breathed in his baby sweet smell and thought, once again, *each precious moment like this* was worth all the sacrifices she had made to be with her son.

"Nargess…" She had to ask, "Is there any more news?"

Nargess took a deep breath. She frowned. "The servants are all worried, khanoum. Nur overheard the generals talking about a meeting that's supposed to take place at the university tomorrow. They're sending soldiers to interrupt the meeting. Abu-Khan wants them to teach the dissidents a lesson."

A chill ran through Olivia. *Teach them a lesson.* That meant bloodshed. "What about Rashid? Have you heard when he's coming? Will he be staying in the palace?"

"His flight is arriving this evening, khanoum, but I don't know if he's coming to the palace." The girl was nearly breathless with the importance of her information. "Abu-Khan told the servants they were *not* to prepare a room for him."

"Does anyone know why he's coming?" Olivia asked. *Is he coming for me?*

"Nur says it's because of the unrest. He thinks Rashid may be planning to go to the meeting tomorrow."

Of course. He was coming because of the political problems, not because of her. If he did go to that meeting, *he would be in danger.*

"You know what?" she said to Nargess, "I've changed my mind. I'd like you to put Jamal down for his nap and feed him when he wakes up."

"Yes, khanoum." Jamal's eyes were drooping. He barely seemed to notice the transfer back into the arms of his nanny. When he was once more resting on her hip, Nargess carried him down the hall to his room.

Olivia had to warn Rashid not to go to that meeting.

She paced the length of the room. How could she get word to him? Where would he go when he got to Behruz? His old friend Reza would know. She had to find Reza, and she had to hurry. Her old method of escaping from the palace, the one she'd used when she was a teenager, depended on her being in the laundry by noon. She had only fifteen minutes.

She grabbed her *chador* and raced along the carpeted hallway to the spiral stairway. She clutched the chador to her heart that was thudding with fear and determination. *Rashid must not attend that meeting.*

The smell of bleach and detergent greeted her in the laundry. There were two workers on duty: Mina, an older woman who'd worked there since Olivia first came to the palace, and a younger girl who was new. Mina probably remembered how Olivia escaped in the past, but she behaved as if a visit to the laundry by the sultan's sister-in-law was a routine occurrence. She introduced Olivia to the new girl, and then returned to her work. Olivia asked about Mina's grandchildren and made small talk with both women until their shift ended. When the two workers donned their chadors, Olivia did the same, draping the large semi-circle of cloth over her head and clutching it in front of her nose and mouth to hide the lower half of her face. Four workers from the cleaning crew joined them as they walked toward the servants' exit, so there were seven women, all hidden in their cocoons of fabric, by the time they approached the guard. Some of the women looked at Olivia with curiosity, but they said nothing. With a flap of fabric pulled over her eyes, she cleared the guard station, just as she had done when she was younger. Outside, the women dispersed without saying a word.

Olivia's step was lighthearted in spite of the urgency of her mission. *Freedom.* The open sky, the crisp air, and the anonymity that was hers thanks to the chador all made her feel carefree again. The smell of meat and spices drifted from a kebab vendor's stand on Karush Street, which was choked as usual with cars, trucks, motorcycles and donkey carts.

****

"I'm the sultan's nephew," Rashid explained.

The soldier shifted from one foot to the other. "You're not on the list, *agha.*"

Not on the list? Since when did he need to be on a list? The guards had always known him. Everyone in the palace had known him. He'd only been gone two years, but now he had to be on a list? "Nur is still the sultan's personal assistant, isn't he? Call him."

The guard picked up a phone. After a minute, he told Rashid, "Agha Nur is coming to the guard station to accompany you into the palace."

Soon Nur was approaching along a path that skirted the palace lawn, walking stiffly, taking small, careful steps. He'd always been short and slender, but now, shriveled and bent with age—he must be about eighty—he was no bigger than Rashid's eleven-year-old cousin. Rashid felt guilty for staying away so long.

Nur greeted him with a formal bow, but Rashid

refused to follow his lead. He hugged his old friend, being careful not to crush bones that seemed terribly fragile.

There were tears in the old man's eyes when Rashid ended the hug. "Welcome Agha Rashid. We were not expecting you until this evening."

"Well, as you can see, I am here now. I didn't expect to be greeted by a battalion of soldiers."

The old man sighed. "These are not normal times."

"Can we go into the palace? Can I see my uncle?"

"I don't think you should, Agha Rashid. The sultan is very occupied. Khanoum Olivia is missing."

Rashid's heart lurched; he couldn't breathe. "What? When?" *Was he too late?*

"It's only been an hour or so, but she's not in the palace and no one knows where she has gone. The Sultan is afraid she's been kidnapped by the rebels."

"Do you think that's possible?"

"I'd say it's unlikely. The instructions she gave the prince's nanny made it sound as if she was *planning* to go somewhere. As you and I both know, she has escaped from the palace for little adventures in the past. That could be what she has done today, but no one knows where she goes."

Rashid took a determined breath. "*I* know."

He arranged for one of the guards to take his suitcase into the palace, and then he headed back toward the busy street to find a taxi. He prayed to his Christian mother's god, *please let her be safe; don't let me be too late,* and then, for good measure, to his father's god too: *Allah…*

****

Olivia had a sense of homecoming as she walked

5

down the tree-lined street toward Reza's home. She was in the neighborhood where Rashid lived as a child before his mother took him to California. He'd brought Olivia here many times when they were younger, and she came by herself sometimes, but it had been years now since she'd snuck out of the palace for a few hours of freedom.

She bought three apples at the produce store and went next door to the shop she and Rashid used to call "the plastic store." Inside, she became a child again, full of wonder at the bright, gaudy objects around her. There were spoons, bowls, sieves, buckets, toys, stools, fly swatters, and hundreds of other items, all plastic, many faded with age and dusty, stacked on shelves and hanging in clusters from the ceiling. She bought a red shopping bag for herself and a green truck for Jamal and then continued on to find Reza, who would be at work in the pharmacy that occupied the ground floor of his house.

She reached the butcher shop across the street from Reza's and was waiting for a break in the traffic when a bicycle swerved in front of her, forcing her to jump back.

"*Bebakshid,* excuse me," the turbaned young rider shouted over his shoulder. He swerved again, this time into the side of an old Volkswagen van parked at the curb.

"Come back here," a woman's voice shouted in English from inside the vehicle, but the bicycle was disappearing around the corner. Olivia approached the van, and a small group of Behruzis who'd seen the incident approached with her.

"There doesn't seem to be any damage," Olivia

said. The side of the van was scratched and dented, but none of the marks looked recent.

The woman glanced at Olivia's shopping bag and at her feet, which were wearing American sport sandals. "Are you American?"

Olivia shifted the chador so her whole face was visible. "Yes, I am."

"There's an American here," the woman said to the man sitting in the driver's seat. He leaned across the woman to study Olivia.

She stared back at the couple. They looked like middle-aged hippies, with long, unkempt hair, loose ethnic shirts, and strands of beads hanging from their necks.

"What are you doing covered up like a native?" the woman asked.

Olivia laughed. Any woman who'd spent any time at all in the Middle East would understand. "I wear a chador in public to avoid attracting attention."

"Oh. Do you *live* here?"

"Yes." She needed to end this conversation. She'd wasted enough time going to the shops.

"Great. Do you know where we can find a veterinarian? We picked up a puppy in Nepal, and there's something wrong with him."

"I'm sorry, I have no idea if there even is a veterinarian in Behruz City. If you want to wait a minute, I'll ask one of the shopkeepers."

"Dammit, he's going to be sick again," the man said. "Get him out of here." The door opened and a small brown bundle of fur was deposited on the curb.

The puppy heaved several times and threw up a mass of wriggling white worms.

The Behruzis watching the scene all took a step back, covering their mouths with handkerchiefs they'd drawn from unseen pockets. The two Americans were discussing the situation in the van.

The man muttered, "I didn't want the damned dog in the first place." He started the engine.

"I'm sorry," the woman said to Olivia. "We have to get to the border tonight."

"Wait," Olivia called, but the van pulled away from the curb and headed down the street.

The puppy lay shivering next to the pile of worms. Olivia took off her chador, wrapped it around him, and picked him up.

Her audience, which had grown, parted to allow her to move across the sidewalk and then formed again in a ring around her when she stopped. She leaned against a ledge in front of the butcher shop under a row of dead chickens that hung from hooks at the edge of the roof. The acrid smell of blood and raw meat filled her lungs as she bent to examine the puppy.

Pleading round eyes peered up at her through a dirty mass of hair that nearly covered the puppy's face. Poor little thing. He was light as a kitten and so thin she could feel his tiny ribs through the soft material.

"*Chee eh? Chee eh*?" everyone asked. "What is it?"

"It's a baby dog. Does anyone want it?"

"She says it's a dog," they repeated. They shuffled and looked nervously at each other, waiting for someone to speak up, but of course no one did. She knew Behruzis thought dogs were filthy animals. No one except the nomads kept them as pets.

"Does anyone know where I can find an animal

doctor?" she asked. They stared back at her.

What could she do? She couldn't take care of a sick puppy, not in the palace.

A new face appeared among the onlookers. It was a man who, with his dark hair and strongly angled face, might have gone unnoticed, but he was taller than the other men, and he was wearing a finely tailored Western suit. His skin was a shade more fair, and his eyes…

His eyes were a deep hazel, so dark they might look black to a casual observer. But a person who had gazed into those eyes with love would know there were flecks of green around the iris, flecks that were encircled by a halo of rich brown.

Olivia knew those eyes. She'd seen them spark green with amusement, she'd seen them darken in anger, and she'd seen them glow liquid brown with passion.

Rashid was back.

Chapter Two

"Olivia." It had been two years since he'd seen her, but she looked the same, still disturbingly beautiful, still impossibly young. He stood gaping at her like the Behruzi men around him.

She had to be twenty-three now, although she could pass for sixteen, at least in her face, in her large, innocent eyes. It was in her body that she'd matured. Everything about her that had been gawky when she was younger—skinny limbs, knobby elbows and knees, long neck—was now pure elegance and grace. She was a swan, a gazelle. Something in his essence reached for her, and he wanted... Never mind what he wanted. Never mind the memories that assaulted him and pulled on his heart. Losing her two years ago had almost killed him. He would never let himself be that vulnerable again. He was here for one reason, to get her out of the country. He must focus on that.

She gazed back at him, her eyes big and round in a face that had gone suddenly pale.

"Olivia." He said it more loudly this time, and everyone turned to look at him. He stepped toward her, but when she cringed away, he stopped. "Are you all right?"

"Yes. It's just such a surprise. What are you doing here?"

"I was looking for you. What are *you* doing here?"

She wrinkled her brow as if his question confounded her. He saw her as the circle of Behruzis must see her. He wondered, as they must be wondering, how this tall, green-eyed foreign girl with golden hair and tight-fitting jeans happened to be standing in front of the butcher shop, pale and bewildered, holding a plastic shopping bag and a chador.

"Please move along," Rashid said to the others. "I'll take care of the young woman." They dispersed, glancing over their shoulders as they shuffled off. Rashid stepped forward to face Olivia. "What are you doing here dressed like that? Why don't you have your hair covered?" *What are you afraid of?*

She stood there with her chador clutched to her breast, her eyes dazed and round. Something was wrong; this wasn't a carefree jaunt. It occurred to him that she might bolt like a frightened fawn. If she pulled the chador over her head, she could lose herself among the other women on the sidewalk.

Be careful, he said to himself. *Go slowly*. And so he softened the urgency in his voice. "What are you doing here?"

"I *was* wearing a chador." She lifted the fabric to show him it was right there in her arms.

"Well good. Why aren't you wearing it now? Why are you here? How did you leave the palace?"

There was a glimmer of the old impish Olivia in her voice when she answered. "I snuck out like I did when I was younger. Abu-Khan will never miss me."

"I'm sorry, but you're wrong about that. The whole palace is in an uproar looking for you."

"Oh no!" The blood drained from her face. "Oh, I must get back. Abu-Khan will be furious!"

Could she actually be *afraid* of Abu-Khan? "I'm sure he's more worried than angry. I'll let him know you're okay." He took out his cell phone and dialed Nur's number. After a moment, he said, "Tell the sultan she's all right. Tell him I'll have her back shortly." He put the phone back in his pocket. "Okay, let's get you to the palace. I'll find a taxi."

"No." She sounded like the stubborn adolescent she'd once been. "No. I have something I have to take care of. You go to the palace and calm Abu-Khan down. I'll return as soon as I've finished with my business."

As if he could walk away and leave her there alone. "What is your business, Olivia? Can I help?"

A camel loped down the street led by a barefooted man wearing a turban and loose nomad clothing. Olivia watched the camel for a moment before answering. "Well, yes, actually, maybe you can."

"What can I do?"

"The problem is that I have this little guy." She separated the folds of the fabric to reveal the large, frightened eyes of a brown puppy. "He's sick. I need to get him to a veterinarian. Do you know where I can find one?"

"What? Where did you get a puppy?"

She explained, in a disjointed story he could barely follow—about a boy on a bicycle...hippies...vomit...worms.

A sick puppy! He'd been thinking she had some deep, terrible problem, something to do with her life in the palace or maybe something to do with the revolution brewing in Behruz. But no, it was a puppy. He could help with that. The knowledge made him feel powerful and heroic, as it always had. And that made him feel the aching pull of desire, a feeling she'd made it clear two years ago he had no right to feel.

"So do you know where I can find someone to help him?"

"Yes, I think I do, but we should return to the palace first."

"No, not until I've seen to the puppy."

He didn't dare argue with her. She was willing to accept his help; that was a start.

"All right, we'll take him to Reza. He'll know what to do. We have to hurry though. Abu-Khan will have my hide if I don't get you back quickly."

"I was on my way to see Reza, actually. I wanted him to get a message to you. I was worried about you."

What? "*You* were worried about *me*?"

"Yes. I was afraid you might be going to a meeting at the university tomorrow."

He could hardly believe what he was hearing. Only a few people knew about the meeting. "How did you hear about that?"

"Oh Rashid, Abu-Khan has spies all over the city. Don't underestimate him."

"So Abu-Khan told you about the meeting?"

"No, the servants did. One of them overheard…"

"The servants. Of course. They hear everything. They could probably run the country by themselves."

"Are you going to the meeting?" she asked.

"I might. Do you know if Abu-Khan plans to interfere with it?"

"Yes, Rashid. He's sending soldiers. They're supposed to *teach the dissidents a lesson.*"

"Well, thank you. I'm sure your warning will save

lives."

He pulled out his cell phone and called one of the organizers of the meeting to tell him the location would have to be changed. When he'd returned his phone to his pocket, he nudged Olivia with his hand at her back. "Okay then, let's take care of this puppy." They crossed the street.

"Rashid, Rashid," the pharmacist said when they entered his shop. He planted a kiss on each of Rashid's cheeks. "Welcome. Who is this lovely young woman with you?"

"This is Olivia Stevens, my uncle's sister-in-law. You remember her, don't you? She has a sick puppy. I was wondering if you might have some medicine for him."

"Hello, Khanoum Stevens." Reza took Olivia's hand and gave her a smile that was all sympathy and kindness. "Yes, I do remember. You are the poor little orphan who came to live in the palace after your parents died."

"Well, yes, I spent summers here with my sister, Karen."

"I remember the last time you were here. The two of you sat and talked in the garden."

He gave Rashid a knowing smile. He must have guessed they'd done more than just *talk*. "And now your sister is gone. What a sad loss it's been for our country, for the sultan, for you, and for that dear baby boy, our beloved little prince. We will never forget our beautiful American sultana."

He motioned to a large framed picture on the wall above the door of his shop, a formal portrait of the royal family taken shortly before Karen died. It showed Abu-

Khan in his military uniform, standing proudly behind Karen, who sat holding the baby. Rashid had seen copies of the picture at the airport, and Olivia had no doubt seen it in public buildings all over the city. She glanced at it and winced. It would be a sad reminder of her sister.

Reza released Olivia's hand. "Yes, yes, yes, I remember when Rashid first brought you to my shop."

Rashid remembered too. It had been Olivia's first summer in Behruz. She'd been lonely and grieving the loss of her parents, but Karen had been too busy with her glamorous life as the sultana to spend time with her little sister. Rashid did what he could to help make Olivia's stay in Behruz interesting. She'd seemed like a child to him—she was thirteen, and he was sixteen—but he was lonely too. They explored the palace and played cards in the evening, and he brought her to his old neighborhood to shop and visit Reza.

Reza studied her. "You were such a skinny little thing." He gave Rashid a sly smile. "But she's become quite a beauty, hasn't she?"

For some reason Reza's familiarity with Olivia irritated Rashid. Reza wouldn't talk like that if Olivia were a Behruzi woman. And he wouldn't have taken her hand either. Reza was probably just trying to be "with it" and "modern" according to his idea of what that meant to his American friends. "Yes, but we're here to see about the puppy, not to review the young lady's charms."

"Of course. The puppy. Tell me what seems to be wrong with him."

Olivia described what she'd seen, and the pharmacist nodded. "Round worms. I have what he needs. Let me see the little guy. I'll have to weigh him." He put on gloves and took the puppy, still wrapped in the chador, into his own large hands. He disappeared into the back of the shop and came back with two capsules. He stuffed one of them down the puppy's throat and told Olivia to administer the second one in two weeks.

A few minutes later, Rashid and Olivia were sitting beside each other in the back seat of a taxi on their way to the palace.

Rashid was suddenly tongue-tied. He'd waited two years. Now, when he finally had a chance to talk to Olivia, she had a wall around her. She was staring out the window of the taxi; she seemed angry. Why would *she* be angry with *him*?

He'd never had any trouble talking to her before. They could talk about *anything*. Every summer when they met again at the palace they'd rush at each other, eager to share all the details of their lives apart.

When the taxi had gone a few blocks, she turned toward him. "I read about your company in The New York Times."

What? "Really?"

Apparently she wanted to keep the conversation impersonal. That was the opposite of what he wanted. He wanted to get personal. He wanted answers. But for now he would follow her lead.

Olivia had always liked hearing about his work. He'd talked about it when he was still in college, when he and one of his friends started translating documents from Farsi to English to earn extra cash. She'd heard all the details as the business grew after they graduated, when they recruited translators who knew other Middle

Eastern languages and then when they started writing software to translate and decode encrypted documents.

"Yes, it was mentioned in relation to some foiled terrorist plot."

Really? In The New York Times? "Well, there have been several attacks averted. I'm not sure which one would have been mentioned in the newspapers."

The street was even more congested than usual, and progress was slow. The puppy wheezed a sigh, and Olivia opened the chador to study him. Her eyes were tender and soft.

She'd looked at Rashid like that once.

But not now. What was wrong?

"How's your mother?" she asked.

His mother? She'd never even met his mother. Was that all she could think to ask after they'd been apart for two long years? With all the questions that lay between them?

Okay. He said his mother was fine. She was still living in San Francisco. His older sister had just had another baby, so his mother was staying with her for a while.

She mumbled another question, her voice so soft he couldn't hear. She was looking down at her fingers, which were busy making little pleats in the fabric of the chador.

"What?"

"How is Shamsi?"

Shamsi? Did Olivia think he was still with Shamsi? Did she think he could have stayed with Shamsi after what happened between *them*? Surely someone had told her…

"Shamsi is fine. She recently became engaged to

one of my friends from college."

"Oh." It was a whisper. It was a gasp.

It seemed she had cared, at least a little. So why hadn't she gotten in touch with him? Why hadn't she returned his calls?

He tried to make eye contact with her, but she turned toward the window again. Traffic was at a near standstill and there were more soldiers. "Livie, can we talk about what happened two years ago?"

She stiffened. Her hand tightened into a fist around the fabric. She didn't answer.

The image crossed his mind again of her as a frightened fawn. How could he break through the wall between them? It felt like a thick fortress right now. He would have to be patient.

He touched the shopping bag that lay between them. "So, do you have to do your own shopping now?"

"No, I just made a few quick stops."

"Did you go to the plastic store?" he asked.

A spark of his old Livie flashed in in her eyes. "Yes of course."

He smiled, and she almost did. "I remember how much you loved that store. Do you make these little forays into town often?"

"No I haven't done it in years. I have a job now. I'm a teacher. But maybe you knew that?"

"No, no one mentioned it. Where do you teach?"

"At the American Academy. I teach music. Well, I did. The school's been closed for two months because of the political problems." She paused. "Did you see Jamal at the palace?"

Jamal? Oh yes, Abu-Khan's son. "No. I didn't make it past the guard station. I wasn't made to feel very welcome."

"I don't suppose you were," she muttered. "Why did you come back?"

He asked himself the more important question: *why had it taken him so long to come back?*

Pride.

This was not his first time back. He'd come once before, two months after they made love, but she'd refused to see him then, and that had hurt more than he could bear. He should have tried harder. He didn't know what problem she was facing, but she'd dealt with it alone long enough. "I was concerned about the political situation. I was worried about my uncle, and I was worried about you."

"I'm fine," she said, her voice quaking.

Yeah, right, she was fine. He couldn't hide his sarcasm when he answered, "So I see."

They were about five blocks from the palace, and traffic had come to a complete stop. There were dozens of army jeeps on the street and hundreds of soldiers on the sidewalk.

"What do you want me to do?" the taxi driver asked. "Should I turn around?"

"No, we have to get to the palace. Maybe if we wait a few more minutes, we'll be able to get through."

Olivia was gazing out the window again. She was so lovely. The smooth curve of her long, neck was irresistible. He reached up and touched it. She stiffened for a second, but then she leaned into his touch. She sighed.

"Livie?" he asked softly.

"You shouldn't have come back," she whispered. He slid his hand down her neck to her shoulder.

Heat surged where his hand rested on her shoulder. The connection was still there. It wasn't just his heat. Energy vibrated between them.

Tears spilled from her eyes. They seemed to accuse him, but of what? Was she trying to punish him? If she was, it was working. Nothing could possibly hurt more than seeing her in pain.

"Oh, Livie." He tried to pull her to him, but she stiffened again.

"Are you sure you don't want me to turn around?" the driver asked.

"No, wait a few more minutes."

He asked Olivia, "Do you think Abu-Khan will be angry?"

"Yes, I imagine he will be."

"Is it going to be a problem?" Was that what she was afraid of?

"No. I can handle it."

The chaos of soldiers and vehicles around them was getting worse, not better. He had to do something. "I'm going to see if there's some way we can get through this mess. I'll be back in a few minutes."

****

Olivia lay back against the seat. The puppy sighed; he was no longer shivering.

Old yearnings tingled from her shoulder where Rashid's hand had rested right to her core. Feelings she didn't want to remember screamed to be acknowledged. Visions from that night two years ago, memories of limbs intertwined, of sweat and heat and *friction*, came unbidden to her mind. Love and resentment pooled together, throbbing in her womb. The most intimate parts of her body recognized that *this man was her mate.*

And he hadn't married Shamsi after all.

Abu-Khan had said something a few weeks after Rashid left, shortly after she found out she was pregnant, that made it sound as if the wedding was imminent. She'd expected, in the weeks and months that followed, to read in the news or hear from Abu-Khan or from the servants that the wedding had taken place, but she never did, and it had been too humiliating to ask—so she'd been left wondering.

Now, finally, she knew. Even though it was too late to matter, her heart sang the news. *Rashid had not married.*

She'd seen the pain on his face when he saw her tears, and for a moment she'd exulted in it. She'd wanted to hurt him—to pay him back for all she'd suffered in the last two years and for the torture she felt now as love and anger and desire churned through her with no hope of relief. But then he'd said her name. He'd said *Livie*, her childhood nickname. Spoken by his lips it was a caress. There had been no pleasure in hurting him after all. He was Rashid. His pain was hers.

He'd said he was worried about her. For two long years, she'd longed and prayed for some sign that he cared, but what difference did it make now?

The sidewalk was filled with soldiers. Did their presence have anything to do with her escape? Of course not. She laughed at herself. It must be because of the political unrest. Abu-Khan would be on the phone with his generals, planning how to return things to normal. Maybe he'd be too busy to talk to her when she got back. No. He'd make time for that. He'd be furious with her for her escape, and he'd be nervous about

Rashid's presence in the country.

If he wasn't on the phone right now then he was probably pacing back and forth while he waited, yelling at poor Nur. Abu-Khan hated waiting more than anything.

He would repeat his threats, but he wouldn't hurt her. He couldn't. She'd lost everything else—her parents, her sister, Rashid, and her freedom—but she still had her son, and that was all that mattered. As long as she didn't tell anyone about Jamal's true parentage, Abu-Khan would let her stay. For some reason it was essential to him that she stay. So let him fume. He seemed almost afraid of her sometimes—some strength in her threatened him—and so he asserted his control in the superficial ways he could. His soldiers escorted her to and from school in his black limousine; his secretary handled her mail and placed her calls for her; and she had no social life. She put up with all that, but when an issue affected Jamal's security and happiness, she would always win.

A young soldier leaning against a wall and smoking a cigarette a few feet away gave her an insolent smile. It was because she was an American and her head was uncovered. She pretended not to notice.

Rashid returned, followed by half a dozen soldiers. One of them, an older man wearing a ridiculously ornate military hat, was familiar to Olivia. He was General Arjangi. She'd met him in the palace.

Rashid opened the door of the taxi and gave money to the driver. "Come on. We'll walk the rest of the way." He took her bag and helped her out of the taxi.

Feeling conspicuous in her casual American clothes, with her hair loose and uncovered and *blonde*,

Olivia clutched the puppy to her breast and lowered her head.

"Hello, khanoum Stevens," the general said in heavily accented English. Thick-soled boots and the tall hat added to his height, but still she towered over him.

"Hello, General." She gave him a weak smile. The soldier who leered at her earlier was now standing at rigid attention, no doubt in deference to the general.

They formed a procession, with two young soldiers in front, then the general, then Olivia and Rashid, and three more soldiers at the rear. The crowds dispersed magically in front of them, allowing speedy progress.

The younger soldiers remained behind while Olivia, Rashid, and the general passed through the gate and under the three marble arches that led to the palace's main entrance. It was a relief to be away from the curious eyes of the soldiers.

Nur was waiting for them at the entrance. He sent her a quick look of sympathy before addressing the general. "Thank you, General Arjangi, for bringing her back to us. The sultan will be grateful to you."

The general's lips curled into a smug smile. Did he think he'd rescued her, or had he captured her? Either way, being the one to bring her back to the palace was likely to be a feather in his cap.

Nur spoke formally, trying, she thought, to make a show of disapproval. "Welcome back, khanoum. Come. I will take you to see the sultan."

"Please, Nur, I'd like a few minutes to myself before I see him." She should change her clothes. And she wanted to do something with the puppy.

"No, khanoum, you must go directly to the sultan. He is waiting."

Rashid had taken her arm when they entered the palace, and he was holding it still. He reached for her other arm and turned her to face him. "Are you going to be all right? He's not going to be too hard on you, is he?"

"No." She forced a note of lightness into her voice. "I'll be okay. I might as well get it over with. Keep the shopping bag for me, please. And would you mind taking the puppy too? It won't help my cause if I show up with him in my arms. Do you think you could get one of the servants to take care of him?"

"Of course," he answered.

She handed him the puppy, still wrapped in the chador.

"Khanoum, the sultan is waiting," Nur reminded her.

"Are you sure you'll be all right?" Rashid asked.

"Yes. Don't worry about me."

He hesitated. "Do you want me to come with you?"

Nur's eyes flashed a warning. Not that she needed to be warned. She knew how Abu-Khan would react if she showed up with Rashid at her side. "No, really, I'll be fine."

"Okay," Rashid still sounded unsure. "I'll talk to you later."

She doubted that. Abu-Khan would make sure they didn't see each other again. And maybe that was for the best. Seeing Rashid was too hard. It reminded her of all she'd lost: her freedom, her dreams, and the wonderful feeling she used to carry with her, even when she was at boarding school in Boston, that there was someone on earth who cared about her. There would be no turning back the clock. She could never forgive him for his cruel behavior two years ago, and she could never tell him about Jamal. It was better not to see him, better to forget.

She followed Nur up the stairs to the second floor and then along the hallway to the north wing. They walked past the guard, through Nur's little vestibule, and into the splendor of Abu-Khan's office. Nur announced, "Khanoum Olivia is here, Sir."

"Thank you, Nur." Abu-Khan was wearing his gray military uniform, with all his medals and ribbons plastered across his chest.

The old man bowed and backed out of the room, closing the door and leaving Olivia standing in front of Abu-Khan's massive desk. She lowered her head trying to look meek and repentant.

Abu-Khan rose, something he'd never done before, his eyes flicking up and down her body, scowling at her jeans.

She stood straight and proud in spite of his perusal. "I *was* wearing a chador."

"Good." He ran his hand through his hair and then patted it back into place. "Sit down, Olivia." He returned to his seat behind the desk, and she sat in an ornate chair across from him. A life-sized portrait of his father, the old sultan, glared from the wall behind him.

A tic quivered in his left eyelid. He seemed to have aged. She remembered how old he'd looked when she first came to the palace. He'd been in his late forties then, but she'd thought him ancient. He'd changed very little in the intervening years, and she no longer considered him old, not usually. He was still imposing, with his thick black hair, now gray at the temples, and his large, hawk-like nose. His eyes were penetrating, intelligent, and cold.

Those eyes accused her now. "I understand you were found in Rashid's old neighborhood."

"Yes. I'm sorry, Abu-Khan." Her head was still bent, hiding any defiance that might show on her face. "I never meant to worry you. It's just that it's been so long since I've been able to go anywhere. I thought I could slip away for an hour or so to wander a little and breathe fresh air."

"There is danger on the streets these days, Olivia, especially for an American, and even more for a member of my household. I keep you here for your protection. You know that."

"Yes, Abu-Khan. I'm sorry. I didn't realize…"

"Have you left for such an excursion before today?"

"No. Well, yes, but it was years ago, and I only did it a few times."

"I see. How did you leave the palace?"

"I just walked out. I wore a chador. The guards thought I was a servant."

"Which guards? Which gate did you use?"

"Please, Abu-Khan, don't make me tell you. I don't want to get anyone in trouble. It was my own fault. No one helped me. No one else should be blamed."

He slammed his flattened palms against the top of the desk. "I will be the judge of that. Which gate did you use? I must insist that you tell me."

"I can't, Abu-Khan. I'm sorry." Her heart was hammering so hard it shook her whole body. This was the first time she'd defied Abu-Khan openly, but she could not betray guards who had never been anything but kind to her.

His hands balled into fists. It seemed he might explode or bellow or even hit her, but instead he curled his lips into a twitching smile and relaxed his hands. "It is of no consequence. You are not my only source of information."

"Please don't punish them, Abu-Khan."

"How were you going to return?"

"I could have used any gate. The guards all know me. They wouldn't question my return to the palace."

"I see." He paused. His military mind was no doubt plotting logistics. There would be new instructions for the guards by the end of the day.

He continued asking questions. Where had she gone? What had she done? How long had she been away? She told him everything, even about the puppy. When she was done, he stood and came to stand over her.

"What about Rashid? Was your meeting with him planned?" He loomed over her. His eyes were lasers, watching her face.

"No. I had no idea he would be there. He brought me back as soon as we'd taken care of the puppy."

"Did you tell him anything?"

"About Jamal? No, of course not. I would never say anything, Abu-Khan."

"Good. You haven't forgotten, have you, what will happen if he finds out?"

"No." As if she ever could. "But what if Rashid sees Jamal? What if he sees the resemblance?" She'd always fantasized that he would.

"He won't! There is no resemblance! The boy looks like every other fat-faced, half-European baby. Rashid will not recognize him. Don't try to trick me,

Olivia. There is only one way Rashid can learn that Jamal is his son. If he finds out, I will know who is to blame."

He returned to the chair behind his desk. He sat for a minute, staring at her, his eyes calculating and cold. "I don't like having to threaten you, Olivia. You gave the boy up of your own free will. You signed the adoption paper; it was all legal. You went along with our plan to let the world believe Karen and I were the natural parents. I must have an heir. If you ever betray me, I'll make sure you never see the boy again. I need to make sure you understand."

"Yes, Abu-Khan, I know." She'd heard this threat a hundred times before.

She remembered the state she'd been in when she signed that wretched paper: newly pregnant, suffering from morning sickness, abandoned by Rashid, depressed, scared, and alone. Abu-Khan and Karen had been relentless in their pressure. Would the decision really be considered to have been made *of her own free will*? Would the paper stand up in a court of law? Probably not in the U.S., but here in Behruz, Abu-Khan was the law.

It had taken less than a minute to sign the adoption paper. Just a few seconds, really. A few seconds that changed her life forever. Her regret was as deep as her love for Jamal, but she didn't dwell on regret. Jamal was still with her. That was what was important now.

Abu-Khan cleared his throat. "All right. Now then, you obviously have not understood the seriousness of the political situation."

"You haven't told me much about it."

"Yes, I realize that. I didn't want to worry you. I

was hoping to have the situation under control by now, but unfortunately, things are getting worse."

That he would confide in her about his political problems was the last thing she'd expected.

"I want you and the boy to leave the city for a while, for your own safety," he said. "One of my secretaries is making the arrangements now. You will go to the Summer Palace in eastern Behruz—the place where you hid with Karen when you were pregnant."

She could scarcely believe she was being offered a respite from the dreariness that surrounded her here. She loved the beauty and serenity of the Summer Palace.

"What about you?" she asked. "Is it safe for you to stay?"

"I am touched by your concern, Olivia. I hope it means you are not as indifferent to me as you appear. In fact, there is danger here. I will be moving to the old fortress south of the city."

He hoped what?

Oh God, did he think she was merely *indifferent*? That was hardly the word to describe the loathing she felt for the man. She bowed her head again. She didn't want him to see the disdain that must certainly be showing on her face. "When do I leave? How long will I be gone?"

"You will leave in about two days, and you'll stay until the rebels have been squashed. I am hoping it will be accomplished in a matter of weeks, but I cannot be certain."

Abu-Khan leaned toward her over his big desk, watching her reaction to this news.

Look meek. Sound meek. "Thank you, Abu-Khan."

"It is nothing. I want you and the boy to be safe. I don't want you to be unhappy, Olivia. I never wanted that. I thought you would adjust to life in the palace...with me."

Something in his tone, in the way he said "with me," alerted Olivia. She remembered a time when she was young when he'd touched her crudely, frightening her. She rose to her feet.

He flinched. "You may go now, Olivia. You will eat dinner with me tonight. Rashid will be there."

"Yes, Abu-Khan."

"I want you to make an effort with your appearance. Wear one of Karen's dresses. And bring Jamal."

"He'll have eaten already. He eats supper at five."

"It doesn't matter. He can sit with us at the table."

"All right." *Innocent and meek.* She left and hurried down the hall, full of relief that the dreaded interview was over.

Abu-Khan must have decided that, since she hadn't told Rashid about Jamal when she had the chance, it would be safe to let them be in a room together. But why did he want Rashid to join them for dinner?

Jamal was in her room playing with toys on the floor when it was time to get ready for dinner. She had four of Karen's dresses in her closet, but she'd never worn them. She looked at them now. They were exquisite really, but they seemed tainted. Abu-Khan had picked them out and paid for them. There had been something like pride of ownership in his eyes when Karen wore them. Would Olivia see the same look tonight when she showed up wearing one at dinner?

If she did, she would just ignore it. She would be as

amenable as possible for two more days; then she would leave this place.

Chapter Three

Rashid's footsteps were muffled by thick Persian carpets as he made his way up the grand spiral staircase and along the corridor to the north wing on the third floor. The puppy, sleeping in the crook of his arm, let out a whistling sigh.

What if she no longer had the same room? She might have been given a larger one now that she was apparently a permanent resident of the palace. Permanent. How could that be? Why was she still here? The last time he saw her she was getting ready to return to the States to attend Juilliard. She'd been so eager to continue her study of music. Why had she changed her mind?

As always, these questions led to the more important question: why had she run from him after the magical night they spent together? She'd written him a letter, but it had explained nothing.

Had she simply been too young to have lasting feelings for him? Had she been toying with him? She was so beautiful and so talented; she could have any man in the world. Maybe she was waiting for some pale-eyed American to sweep her off her feet.

That thought was fueled by old insecurities. He'd been twelve when his father died and his mother took him and his sisters to live in California. It was shortly after the 9/11 terrorist attack, and sentiment against

Middle Easterners was high. Other children had been cruel to the dark-eyed boy with the Muslim-sounding name. He'd eventually found acceptance, starting when he joined the soccer team, but old scars were still there.

Olivia had never shown the slightest prejudice against anyone for reasons of race or religion. On the contrary, love and compassion emanated from her like warmth from a fire. She treated Nur like a beloved grandfather, and all the servants adored her.

There had to be some reason why she'd rejected him, but none of his speculations made sense. The Olivia he knew would not have offered herself to him the way she did if she didn't have serious feelings. So why had she suddenly refused to talk to him?

Hopefully he would learn more tonight. But he had to tread carefully; he didn't want to make her any more wary than she already was. He couldn't get her out of the country without first gaining her trust.

How was he going to do that? She barely trusted him enough to let him help with the puppy. He reached her room and knocked on the door. After a moment, it opened. It was the right room. Olivia stood in the doorway.

She was breathtaking. He'd never seen her dressed like this before. She was wearing an incredible gown of some shimmering soft material in pale blue. It was tight around the waist and bodice, but everywhere else it was loose and flowing. Her eyes were soft and melting, vulnerable and confused. Her skin was smooth and soft, without a trace of makeup.

Her lips were pursed and uncertain. Her hand was still clutching the doorknob. "What do you want?"

He could scarcely remember his reason for coming

to her room. It had been overridden by an overwhelming urge to kiss those lips, to touch her. Her feminine softness pulled at every cell in his body. "I've brought your bag and your puppy. Can I come in for a minute?"

"Oh." Her eyes shifted uneasily to the empty hallway and then to the corner of the room, to something out of Rashid's sight. "I don't think it's a good idea. I was getting ready to go down to dinner. I…"

She seemed almost too flustered to speak. Why? He wanted to grab her, use force, do anything he had to do to get her out of Behruz, but there would be no sneaking across the border with an unwilling hostage, especially if the border officials had been put on the alert to watch for that hostage.

"I'm sorry, Livie. I need to talk to you. Let me come in for a few minutes, and then we can go down to dinner."

"All right." She let him push his way past her into the room and close the door. "Let me see the puppy first." She reached to take him from Rashid's arm.

"No. I don't think… Your dress—"

"Never mind the stupid dress!" She reached for the puppy, and Rashid let her take him. She was shaking. He felt the tremor on his arm when she slid her hand under the puppy.

What was wrong with her? The outburst about the dress was completely out of character, and it was also impossible to understand. How could she not like such an exquisite dress? There couldn't be a woman alive who wouldn't love the dress.

"He's beautiful." She held the puppy cupped in her

hands against her breasts. "How did you get him clean?"

"A woman named Mina in the palace laundry washed him. She fed him, too, and she's also washing your chador. She said to tell you it will be ready tomorrow." He set the bag on the floor. "She didn't want to touch the puppy, but I gave her fifty tokhans and that changed her mind. How much is fifty tokhans anyway? I'm not used to the new exchange rate."

"It's about twenty-five dollars." A half-smile softened Olivia's face. "It was far too much. She probably doesn't earn that much in a month."

"She did seem quite pleased."

"You were always too generous with the servants. I remember how mad it used to make Abu-Khan."

"Yes, well, avoiding Abu-Khan's anger wasn't always my top priority."

"What kind of dog do you suppose he is?" she asked.

"I would say he's a Lhasa Apso, judging by his long hair and the pompon tail. You said they got him in Nepal, didn't you? I know they raise Lhasa Apsos there."

There was a little thud behind Rashid. Olivia's eyes darted from the puppy to the source of the sound and then to Rashid.

What? He swung around. A baby boy was using the bedpost to pull himself up from the floor.

Olivia went stony still and pale.

He stepped toward her and touched her arm. Her skin was cold. "What's the matter?"

"Oh." She didn't move away from his touch. "This is…" She looked at the boy as if trying to remember his name. "This is Jamal."

The little boy peered solemnly at the two grown-ups.

"Of course, the young heir." Rashid glanced again at the little boy and then turned his attention back to Olivia. Why was she upset?

"He's spotted the puppy. He's never seen one before, except in books." She sat down cross-legged on the plush Persian carpet, adjusted her skirt over her legs, and placed the puppy in her lap.

The boy stood for a moment staring at the puppy, and then he dropped to his knees and crawled to Olivia, never taking his eyes from the bundle of fur in her lap.

When he reached her, he lowered himself to his stomach so he and the puppy were eye to eye. They stayed like that for a while, neither moving, until the baby reached to touch the puppy's nose. When his fingers were an inch from their goal, the puppy let out a little yip and scampered under the bed. Jamal lurched back, surprised, and looked up at Olivia.

"That's a *puppy*, Jamal. He went under the bed. See if you can find him."

The boy crawled eagerly to the bed.

"He's beautiful, isn't he?" she asked Rashid. She raised herself from the floor.

"Yes." Oh God, *she* was beautiful. His heart ached with the beauty of her. How had he gone two long years without seeing her? She was watching him, anxiously studying his every reaction, waiting for something. But what?

Trust me. Tell me what's troubling you.

Her eyes called to him with their frightened appeal. He stepped closer to her, until their bodies were almost touching, and she didn't back away. He reached up and cupped her face with his hands. His thumbs came to rest against the corners of her mouth. "Livie, I'm so sorry."

Why had he said that? He'd never in his life done anything to hurt her, but someone or some circumstance *had* hurt her, and he hadn't been there to protect her. He moved his thumbs across her lips. She stood with her hands at her sides, not encouraging him but not resisting either.

He felt the wetness of tears on her face. He kissed each of her closed eyes, tasting salt, tasting her, wanting her, hating that he wanted her. But wanting her. And wanting to take away the pain or fear or whatever it was that brought those tears. He brought his lips down the slope of her cheek, aching for her lips, but she turned her face away, rejecting the kiss she must have known was coming.

Damn her. For rejecting him. Again. Damn her for making him want to be the hero in her life. Again. While his mind damned her, his heart shrank with fear, knowing her power to hurt him. Meanwhile his libido screamed *never mind all that*. His arms reached for her and drew her against him, and finally, miraculously, she yielded. Her slender body slumped against him, and her arms came up to cling to his neck. A sob sounded in her throat, and her body shook against him.

He tightened his hold, crushing her against his chest, wanting to give her his strength, wanting to possess her, to take her right inside himself. Desire swelled, painful and urgent, but he ignored it. No. *Not that. Not now. Not with her*. She didn't want him, not like that. Still, for some reason she needed him.

He cradled her head against his cheek and stroked her back, letting her cry, waiting until she was calm.

"What's the matter, Livie? You have to tell me."

She clung to him a minute longer, quiet now, and then she lowered her hands to his chest and lightly pushed. "I don't know why I fell apart like that. Please excuse me. It's nothing to do with you."

She was trying to compose herself. He could see her effort to re-erect the barriers that would shut him out. He loosened his grip.

"There's nothing wrong, really," she said. "I should never have let myself…"

Jamal wailed. He was lying on his stomach with his head and shoulders wedged under the bed, apparently stuck. Olivia hurried to where he lay and bent over him.

"Can you lift the bed?" she asked Rashid. She couldn't have done it herself. It was a massive canopy bed, probably one of the eighteenth century pieces Abu-Khan's mother had had brought from France. Rashid used all his strength to raise it so she could rescue the boy. She lifted him off the floor and sat on the edge of the bed, holding him, patting him, whispering soothing words. Soon his sobbing ended.

She was an angel—with her golden hair and that blue dress and with the baby in her arms. Whatever was troubling her was forgotten now; she was all tenderness, all love. She held the baby against her breast with her arms tight around him, and he clung to her. Her lashes were still wet with tears, but her face was serene now.

So that was why she was still in Behruz. Of course. Her sister was dead. Her sister's son needed a mother.

But why had she stayed in Behruz two years ago when she was set to start at Juilliard? There hadn't been an orphaned baby *then.*

Jamal peered at Rashid with an impish determination on his face. He pursed his lips in concentration and then opened them and carefully pronounced the word *pup-pee.*

"Oh, he said *puppy,*" Olivia exclaimed. "That's his first word!" She beamed the carefree, happy smile of the Livie he remembered.

"Puppy?" Jamal formed the word again, this time as a question. He looked around the room and squirmed to get free from Olivia's arms.

Rashid checked under the bed, but the puppy was no longer there, so all three searched the room. Rashid found him curled up in the closet on a terry cloth robe that had fallen from its hook. He was asleep.

"The puppy is sleeping," Olivia said to Jamal. She and the boy knelt to look at the little ball of fur, both with their heads in the closet and their rumps in the air. It was such a lovely sight—the lumpy little diapered bottom on one side, and the round, female bottom beside it. Rashid ached to slide his hand across the filmy blue fabric that fell over the soft shape before him. Raw, male hunger surged in him. And the old protective urge Olivia had always evoked. He was shaking with the power of his feelings and burning with his need for her when Olivia raised herself up from the floor.

"Come on," she said to Jamal. "Let's leave the puppy alone for a while. It's time to go to dinner."

It was time already? Rashid hadn't said any of the things he meant to say. He hadn't even mentioned the political situation or the need for her to leave the country. And now it was time to join Abu-Khan. He'd have to find a way to talk to her after dinner. In the meantime he would find out more about Abu-Khan's plans. Maybe Abu-Khan could be persuaded to make the necessary compromises with the rebels. Maybe there was still hope.

"Will the baby walk or should I carry him?"

"Oh." She hesitated. "I'll carry him. He's a little shy with strangers."

"Let's see, shall we?" He got down on one knee and addressed Jamal. "The puppy is sleeping. We have to go to dinner now, but we can see the puppy again after we eat."

"Puppy," the boy said. He was studying Rashid with eyes wide and curious.

Rashid pointed to the shopping bag. "Was there something in there for a boy?"

"Yes. How did you know that?"

Rashid laughed. "Just a guess. I remember the treasures that can be found in the plastic store."

She reached into the bag and found the green truck.

Rashid took the child into his arms and stood. Before Jamal could protest, he took the toy from Olivia's hand and placed it in the boy's. "That's a *truck*. Can you say *truck*?"

"Puppy," the boy answered.

Olivia and Rashid looked at each other and laughed. For a moment, the barriers were gone, and they were together in the old, easy way. A space in his heart that had been cold and empty for two long years filled with warmth. He would win her trust somehow, and he would convince her to leave with him. He had to.

****

The suspense was over for Olivia. Rashid hadn't recognized his son.

The sight of Rashid and Jamal together, interacting in a way that would be commonplace if they lived as father and son, twisted her heart. Rashid carried Jamal down the wide spiral staircase in an easy, comfortable way. He had nieces and a nephew back in California. He was used to dealing with children. He liked them.

But, no, she mustn't think of Rashid in those terms: as a man who liked children. As a potential father. He hadn't recognized Jamal. There was really no surprise in that. She'd never expected he would.

Still, she'd had her fantasies. And she'd had her fears.

That didn't matter now. It was over. The fantasies could end, and so could the fear of what Abu-Khan would do if Rashid learned the truth. Her future was clear. She would go to the Summer Palace, and she would come back when Abu-Khan said it was time. She would raise her son here in the palace. Alone.

She'd been virtually on her own since she was thirteen years old—relying on herself, making her own decisions, solving her own problems. Nothing had changed.

When they got to the smallest dining room, the one they used for family meals, she took Jamal from Rashid's arms and held him for a moment herself before settling him in his high chair. She sat in the seat next to Jamal, and Rashid sat across from them at the end of a teak table Karen had purchased soon after she became the sultana. Abu-Khan hadn't arrived yet, so they were alone except for the old servant Faizal, who was filling water glasses.

"Jamal has rather odd coloring, don't you think?" Rashid asked.

Oh no, he'd noticed the hair. She'd been helping Jamal drink water from a crystal goblet. Now she took the goblet away and handed him a piece of bread. She waited until Faizal left the room and then whispered to Rashid, "You mean his hair?" It seemed an act of treason to discuss Jamal's hair. "This is not his natural color. Actually his hair is light brown, but Abu-Khan has one of the servants dye it black. He thinks Jamal looks more like a leader with his hair dark."

Rashid chuckled. "Of course. Now that you've told me, I can see it. It's obvious and also quite odd, as I'm sure you know. I'm surprised you permit it."

"You don't know your uncle very well if you think he needs *my* permission to do as he wishes."

Rashid turned sharply toward her. "Oh...I thought... Well, Abu-Khan used to spoil you terribly."

Blood rushed to her cheeks, and tears stung her eyes. When had Abu-Khan or anyone else ever spoiled her? No one had, not since the death of her parents. Except Rashid. "You don't know what you're talking about."

"No, perhaps not." His gaze hadn't wavered from her face. "Tell me, how was your meeting with Abu-Khan this afternoon? Was he hard on you?"

"No. It wasn't too bad."

Faizal opened the door, and Abu-Khan entered wearing a long maroon robe trimmed with gold edging. Olivia and Rashid rose to their feet.

"Rashid, welcome." Abu-Khan stepped to the side

of the table and stood before Rashid, allowing the younger man to kiss him on both cheeks. Then he walked around the table to the side where Olivia stood. "Olivia, my dear, the dress is lovely."

Olivia froze, startled by Abu-Khan's intimate tone. Trapped. She couldn't question him, not in front of Rashid. Rashid's eyes were on her, no doubt analyzing every trace of emotion that crossed her face. Abu-Khan took her hand and raised it to his lips, kissing the palm, all the while glaring at her with cold menace, reminding her of what she had to lose if she didn't play along. Not that she needed reminding. He pulled out her chair and waited for her to be seated. She thanked him as icily as she dared, wiping her hand on her skirt to remove the taint of his kiss.

Rashid's eyes narrowed and his brows lifted when Abu-Khan made his remark about Olivia's dress. He wouldn't guess that this was the first-time Abu-Khan had ever performed any gentlemanly courtesy such as helping with her chair, and this was the first time he'd touched her since the summer when she was fifteen, when he'd hurt and frightened her, tearing her blouse and grabbing her breasts. She'd written him a letter, telling him that if he ever touched her again she'd tell her sister, and he hadn't touched her since.

"Please sit down, Rashid," Abu-Khan said when Olivia was seated, and then he went to his own place at the head of the table. "I presume you've met my son?"

Please don't say anything about Jamal's hair. She should never have mentioned the dye. She should have made sure he understood he was not to bring up the subject with Abu-Khan.

"Yes, he is a fine boy." Rashid's voice was

controlled. He was on guard; he would not betray her.

Dinner, a traditional Behruzi dish of chicken kebab and rice, was served by Faizal and his brother Esmail.

"Is there a room ready for my nephew?" Abu-Khan asked Faizal.

Poor Faizal. According to Nargess, the servants had been told *not* to prepare a room for Rashid. But apparently Abu-Khan had decided he wanted Rashid to stay in the palace after all. Faizal hesitated just a split second and then quickly answered, "Yes, Excellency. Of course, Excellency."

Rashid took a sip from his water glass. "You're very kind, Uncle, but I have made arrangements to stay with a friend."

"As you wish," Abu-Khan replied. "It is of no concern to me."

Olivia toyed with her food and kept quiet, listening in amazement to the men's conversation about the political situation. Although she frequently watched the news on television and she read the local newspaper and The New York Times, she'd heard nothing of the dramatic events they were discussing. She'd always known there was press censorship—or "media supervision" as Abu-Khan called it—but she'd never realized the power that censorship gave to Abu-Khan. Apparently he'd been practicing a little private censorship just for her too, for several issues of the New York Times had been missing from her mail during the last few months.

Why was he allowing her to overhear this conversation with Rashid? He must think that now, with Rashid's visit and with her impending trip, it was inevitable that she'd learn more about the situation. Or perhaps it was part of the little act he was playing for Rashid's benefit, this apparent inclusion of her in matters of government. Whatever his reasons, she was glad of the opportunity to learn more.

Rashid wanted Abu-Khan to make concessions to the rebels. "Uncle, a few reforms might buy you more time. Perhaps some measures to help the poor? Or the release of a few political prisoners?"

Abu-Khan's face reddened. He huffed and sputtered before answering. "My enemies would consider such moves to be a sign of weakness! I will squelch this rebellion by a show of strength, not weakness!"

"Please, Uncle, the threat is serious; there could be bloodshed. You may be in danger yourself." Rashid hesitated; he rearranged the silverware in front of him, clanking it against his plate. "Olivia and your son may be in danger."

Abu-Khan's steaming face colored even more. "Do not question my ability to protect my family! You should worry about yourself. Go back to your easy life in America. If I find out you've had anything to do with the fanatics who threaten me, you will be deported in the blink of a camel's eye. Unless I'm in a bad mood, in which case you will be beheaded."

"I apologize, Uncle. I know how much you love your country. I know what a fine leader you've been. I didn't mean to challenge your wisdom."

"Good." Abu-Khan wiped his napkin across his forehead and upper lip.

Olivia could hardly believe Rashid had deferred to Abu-Khan with such ease. She remembered how he used to enjoy arguing with Abu-Khan when he was younger. He hadn't backed down from his idealistic stands *then*.

"Olivia dear," Abu-Khan's tone was smooth and controlled now, "I am so sorry you've had to listen to all of this nasty business. Please excuse us for discussing it in your presence."

She smiled meekly and ignored his patronizing remark. Jamal threw his truck under the table, and she went down on her hands and knees to retrieve it. Both men paused in their conversation until she returned to her seat. Abu-Khan must be enjoying watching her helplessly play the role of pawn in his game, whatever it was. What must Rashid think? He seemed to be waiting for something from her, as if some unconscious gesture of hers would be the key to a great mystery.

Faizal removed the dinner plates and served the pastries and tea. Olivia kept busy helping Jamal with his pastry in an effort to escape Rashid's penetrating gaze. She hated the two men almost equally in that moment. What did Rashid want from her? What did Abu-Khan have planned for her? And when would this interminable dinner end?

Rashid took a bite of his dessert and then paused with his fork in the air. "I do have one question, Uncle. Please don't be offended by my asking. Surely you can understand why I'm concerned. I was wondering how you plan to keep Olivia and Jamal safe."

Abu-Khan's voice was tight, his face flushed, but he didn't raise his voice. "As I told you before, you need not concern yourself with my family. Olivia and my son will be taken to a safe place."

"I see. Is this what you want, Olivia?"

"Of course it is what she wants," Abu-Khan

thundered before Olivia could speak. "We have discussed it. All has been arranged."

"I see," Rashid said again. He seemed about to say more, but Olivia appealed to him with her eyes and he dropped the subject.

Jamal threw his truck onto the floor again. He was watching Rashid while he did it, apparently expecting a reaction. When Rashid said nothing, Jamal gave him a silly defiant look and carefully pronounced the word *fruck*.

Rashid and Olivia started to laugh, but when they saw Abu-Khan's scowl of disapproval, they squelched their grins.

"What did he say?" Abu-Khan demanded to know.

"I think he said *truck*," Olivia replied as soberly as she could.

This angered Abu-Khan. "He should be learning Farsi, not English. I want you to speak Farsi to him while you are away from the city. When you come back I will arrange for a tutor."

"Yes, Abu-Khan."

Rashid must have seen that her meekness was forced. He hid his mouth behind his hand, but his eyes were laughing. So he thought this cat-and-mouse game was funny? She was exhausted from the strain of navigating Abu-Khan's moods and trying not to reveal too much to Rashid. "Jamal is tired," she said. "If you'll excuse me, I'll take him to bed."

Abu-Khan granted her permission to leave. Rashid retrieved the truck and then stood while she collected Jamal and left the room.

Chapter Four

It was hopeless. Abu-Khan would not hear reason. The two men feigned cordiality for half an hour more, but then Abu-Khan suddenly decided it was time to retire. Rashid pulled out his cell phone and pretended to study his messages until Abu-Khan was out of sight. Then he hurried to the staircase. He had to get Olivia out of the country.

He tapped on her door but didn't wait for an answer. Instead he eased the door open and slipped inside.

She was lying on a chaise lounge in the corner of the room with a mug in her hand. It would be chamomile tea. She'd always liked chamomile tea at bedtime.

"What?" She rose to her feet.

"Shh." Rashid closed the door and crossed the room to stand before her. She was wearing a threadbare flannel nightgown she'd worn as a teenager. "Can't you afford a new nightgown? Or can't you take one of Karen's?" There were probably dozens of fine silk nightgowns still in Karen's dressing room.

"I like this one." She flicked her hand, dismissing the importance of nightgowns. "Why are you here? I'll be in terrible trouble if Abu-Khan finds out you've been in my room."

"I need to talk to you. I won't stay long. There's a

meeting I need to attend." He checked his watch. Damn. He was late already.

And damn, her nipples pushing against the soft flannel were even more tempting than they would have been outlined in silk.

She took a step back from him. "We can talk tomorrow."

"Livie, please. This is important." *Couldn't she trust him just a little?*

"What do you want?" She clenched her hands in front of her breasts. But he could still see her nipples. And he could remember…

No. He had to stay focused. "Can you sneak away from the palace again tomorrow the way you did today?"

"I don't know. Abu-Khan has probably told the guards to watch for me. Why?"

"Can you try? Would they hurt you if they stopped you?"

"Yes, I could try. No one would hurt me. But Abu-Khan has a plan. You don't have to worry about me."

"Right. Tell me, where is he sending you? To the Summer Palace?"

"Yes." She sounded uncertain.

"What makes you think you'll be safe there? The rebels will go there to loot the place; finding you would be a nice bonus."

Fear flashed in her eyes. He didn't like scaring her, but he had to make her listen.

"Don't worry about me." Her voice was barely a whisper. "Abu-Khan will take care of everything."

Rashid grasped her shoulders, pulling her toward him. She had to listen to *him*. She had to trust *him*.

"Don't be naive, Olivia. Abu-Khan is refusing to face facts; he can't stand to have his authority challenged. The Summer Palace is not a safe place. Nowhere in this country is safe, and this palace is the most dangerous place of all. You have to leave."

She tried to turn away, but he tightened his grip. "No," she gasped. "No, I can't leave Behruz."

"Why?"

"Please, you're hurting me."

He looked at his hands. They were hurting Livie. He pulled them away. "I'm sorry."

"I don't need your help. I appreciate your concern, but Jamal needs me. I can't leave him. Please go. Please leave me alone."

The boy. Of course. She was like a mother to him. "Livie, we can take him with us."

"No, I couldn't. Abu-Khan would be furious. No."

"Listen, if you love that little boy, then get him out of this country. The rebellion will get bloody. You can come back when peace has been restored." He took her by the shoulders again, more gently this time. "Trust me, Livie." *Trust me like you used to.* His hands slid up to stroke her neck and then her cheeks and temples. She turned to him. She sighed. She nuzzled her head into his hands. Her jaw relaxed; her lips parted. He moved his thumb across her lower lip. His heart pumped love and lust through his body. *He would break down her defenses. He had to.* He would save her.

But he had to get to the damned meeting. He had to try to convince the rebel leaders to give Abu-Khan more time. "I have to leave. I'm meeting with some of the rebels tonight, and then there's another meeting tomorrow, the one that was supposed to be at the university. I want you to leave with me after that meeting."

"No Rashid. Abu-Khan would never forgive us if we took Jamal." He would never forgive *her*.

"I'll send him a letter. I'll explain everything. I'll take full responsibility. He may be upset at first, but once he understands what's happening, he'll be glad you and Jamal fled to safety."

He had to get to the meeting. Oh God why did he have to leave *now*? "If anything changes, if I find out at one of these meetings that there's some hope of a peaceful settlement, I'll let you know, but it isn't likely. Please let me help you, Livie. You must leave the country before things turn violent." He opened the door. "I'll contact you tomorrow after the meeting."

****

Wait. Don't leave. She didn't know what to do. Maybe she should tell him about Jamal. She couldn't think fast enough.

He slipped through the door and closed it quietly behind him. *Wait.*

He was gone.

Could she leave with him? Should she? Living with Abu-Khan's threats and submitting to his domination for two years had made her unsure of her own judgment.

She'd often thought of trying to escape with Jamal but had never come up with a feasible plan. One thing she knew: if she ever managed to escape, Abu-Khan would try to find her. And if he found her he'd take Jamal. He was *a sultan*. He had *power*. And he had a legal document, *signed by her*, giving him the right to execute that power.

Her ideas about how she might live in hiding from Abu-Khan were sketchy. She had one friend she knew she could count on to help: a teacher from her boarding school days in Boston. She would go to her. Together they would figure something out.

That was as close as she'd ever come to having "a plan." It wasn't much. Trying to escape would be a huge gamble.

Could she trust Rashid? Could he help her, even if he didn't know all the facts? Could she trust herself not to *tell* him all the facts?

She lay in bed, unable to sleep, questions and doubts spiraling in her mind. What should she do?

A whimpering sound woke her the next morning. The puppy was beside the bed, gazing up at her and wagging his funny little tail. A dim light came from the small window behind her. It was dawn.

She was surprised to realize she'd slept. She'd thought her mind was going to torture her all night with fear and indecision, with memories of what it was like to be in Rashid's arms, with questions about how *he* felt when he held her, and with anger at herself for *caring* what he felt. Rashid's predictions about the political situation were probably right, but Abu-Khan would find her if she left, and he'd bring Jamal back to Behruz.

The puppy had peed on a towel on the floor in the bathroom. "Smart puppy," she said to him. She dropped the towel into the bathtub to be rinsed out later, threw a spare chador over her nightgown, picked up the puppy, and headed downstairs. There were soldiers everywhere. Each of them snapped to attention when she approached and then watched curiously out of the corner of his eye until she was out of sight.

She took the puppy to the courtyard by the kitchen and let him run free for a few minutes; then she went to the kitchen where she found that her breakfast and Jamal's had already been sent up to her room. She showed the puppy to one of the kitchen helpers and together they brainstormed what might be an appropriate breakfast for him. A few minutes later she was on her way back upstairs with a puppy-sized serving of cooked lamb.

She held him for a while after he ate, marveling at the speed of his recovery. Poor thing. What would become of him? She should have found out his name from the hippies. She didn't want to name him—that would make her feel responsible for him. How could she take care of a puppy when she didn't even know how to take care of herself and Jamal?

She put him down on the floor and opened her closet to choose clothes for the day. What would she be doing? Abu-Khan thought she was preparing for a trip to the Summer Palace, but Rashid had her almost convinced she should leave the country.

How would Rashid get a message to her? And when? And what would she say?

She'd just put on a pair of jeans when the intercom squawked. It was Nur calling to say Abu-Khan wanted to see her in his office. Immediately.

Okay. She grabbed a pink ruffled blouse—Abu-Khan would like that—but she didn't take time to change the jeans.

"Wish me luck," she said to the puppy who peering at her from inside the closet. "I'll be right back. Don't make a mess."

When she opened the door, she found a soldier

waiting in the hallway. "I will escort you to the sultan's office," he said.

"Why? What's going on?"

"I am to escort you," he replied.

Three soldiers were standing at attention outside Jamal's room. Olivia hesitated at his door.

"The sultan is waiting," her escort reminded her.

"Just a second." She spoke to one of the soldiers standing at Jamal's door. "Would you please tell the prince's nanny that his breakfast is in my room?"

"Yes, khanoum." The man tapped on Jamal's door. Olivia's escort marched her away before Nargess answered.

A dozen soldiers stood at attention in front of Abu-Khan's office. One knocked on the door and announced her arrival, and Nur led her into the inner office. Abu-Khan, in his military uniform, was sitting at his desk studying a chart of some kind.

"Olivia. Sit down. I am very busy. We are going this afternoon to the old fortress. You will come with me. It is not safe now to travel to the Summer Palace. You can go later. Now you will stay with me."

Her prison door clinked shut. She would stay with Abu-Khan.

"I must take care of this insane rebellion," he said. "There are only a few rebels, you know. Rashid thinks there is a large number, but he is wrong. I have not been harsh enough, but I know now what I must do. I am in control. You will see."

Olivia's heart was galloping. She'd never seen him like this. "Please listen to Rashid. He wants to help you maintain peace."

His hands moved restlessly across the surface of

his desk, and his eyes darted nervously from Olivia's face to the corners of the room. "Enough. Do not speak Rashid's name again! He doesn't understand the politics of this country! And *you* know even less. This is not your concern. I will take care of everything. Do you hear me?"

"Yes, Abu-Khan. I'm sorry, it's just that I thought maybe you could—"

"I said enough!" He drew a rasping breath; his hands balled into fists on the desk. "Now sit down. I have not brought you here to speak of politics. There's something else."

There was an odd hesitation in his voice. She sat quickly in a chair across the desk from him.

"Olivia, I want to marry you."

"What!"

His eyelid twitched. "I see this has come as a surprise to you, but trust me, I have thought about it for a long time. I've waited long enough. It's been almost a year since Karen died. My people would not expect me to wait any longer. You will be Jamal's mother, Olivia. Think of it. He will call you *mother*."

"Abu-Khan, I couldn't possibly—"

"No!" He pumped his fists where they lay on the desk. "No, don't answer me now. We won't be able to be married until things are back to normal. We will not speak of it until then."

"But…"

"No!" He screamed the word. Nur and the soldiers must have heard it through the wall, but they wouldn't interfere. "Forget Rashid. He doesn't want you any more, and even if he did, you can never be with him, not unless you're willing to say goodbye to Jamal forever."

He emphasized the word *forever*. His eyes glittered with menace. There was no point in arguing with him. He was giving her time; nothing would happen until his political problems were resolved. She would think of something before then.

He walked around his desk to stand above her, glaring with fevered, moist eyes. "I want you to wear this, Olivia. It is a difficult time for me, and I may be in danger. It will mean a great deal to me to know you're wearing it."

"But Abu-Khan…"

"Shut up! Do not speak!" He wrenched her hand away from the arm of the chair and held it in a crushing grip while he forced an emerald ring onto her finger. "You should be grateful for this offer. I could send you back to your own country and find a nice Behruzi girl to raise your bastard son, but I want you."

Olivia was stiff with terror. Abu-Khan jerked her from the chair into his arms and kissed her, forcing his tongue between her lips. She tasted tobacco and madness. He brought his hand down to touch her intimately between her legs, still holding her in an iron grip with his other hand. "You will not wear clothes such as these when you are my wife." His hand closed, pinching her flesh painfully through the heavy fabric of her jeans.

She twisted away, and he released her, allowing her to fall back into the chair.

He returned to his chair, looking exhausted. He buried his face in his hands for a moment and then gave her a grimace of appeal. "I'm sorry, Olivia. I don't want to hurt you, but you shouldn't resist me. I'll be gentle when we're married, I promise. Karen was happy with me, and you will be too. I'm so tired now. I haven't slept. There's so much to do. It will be all right later."

"May I go now?"

"Yes, you may go." He pressed a button on the phone and picked up the receiver. He told someone, probably Nur, "Tell the guard Miss Stevens is ready to return to her room."

Olivia jumped to her feet. She reached the door just as the soldier came in.

"The soldier has been instructed to watch you, Olivia. You are to stay in your room. This is for your own safety."

For her safety. Right. She looked back at Abu-Khan from the doorway. So now she understood his behavior at dinner last night. He wanted to make the engagement he would soon be announcing seem plausible. He was a conniving bully. How could she have let him dominate her for so long? A new resolve rushed through her veins like high-octane fuel. An old confidence surged.

You will not win, arrogant, little man.

She stood squarely before him, no longer trying to appear meek. "I'll need to have Jamal with me, Abu-Khan."

"Of course." He told the soldier, "Miss Stevens is permitted to have my son with her."

"Yes, Excellency," the soldier replied.

Please, let Rashid be safe, Olivia prayed as she followed the young soldier toward the stairs. Please don't let Abu-Khan's soldiers find out where the meeting is being held.

She would leave with Rashid. She couldn't

possibly stay now. But how would he contact her with a soldier guarding her door?

Her mind raced, trying to deal with the practicalities of the situation. If she did by some miracle manage to escape the palace and meet up with Rashid, how could they get out of the country? Did Rashid realize Abu-Khan had her passport? Did he know Abu-Khan would be trying, with all his seemingly unlimited power, to prevent their escape?

The sound of crying greeted her when she and the soldier reached the hallway on the third floor. It was Jamal wailing his desire to see the puppy. Poor Nargess was beside herself trying to figure out what he wanted. Olivia explained and then took Jamal to her room. The soldiers who'd been standing outside Jamal's room followed in a little procession.

Olivia opened the door and they got a glimpse of the puppy.

"*Chee eh? Chee eh?*" the soldiers asked each other.

"It's a baby dog," she explained before closing the door.

She put Jamal down beside the puppy and walked across the room to the small window. Soldiers were running across the large expanse of grass toward the main gate. *Please don't let it be too late. Let me get out of here in time.*

A knock at the door made her jump. Rashid? *Please, let it be Rashid.* She stepped around the boy and puppy to open the door.

It was Mina from the palace laundry. "I've brought your chador, khanoum."

Mina extended her hands to offer Olivia the chador. A piece of paper stuck out from between its folds. Mina held it out of sight of the soldiers, but they wouldn't have noticed anyway. They were trying to peek around the women to get a glimpse of the puppy.

"Thank you very much," Olivia said.

Mina released the chador into Olivia's hands. "The laundry man said to ask if you have anything you want washed today."

There were no men in the palace laundry, as far as Olivia knew. Mina must be referring to Rashid. The paper must be a note from him, and Mina was giving Olivia a chance to send a message back. "Yes, I think I do. Wait a minute while I check."

She took the chador and crossed the room to the bathroom, where she took the paper into trembling hands.

The soldiers on your floor will be called away about fifteen minutes after you receive this note. Be prepared to run as soon as you hear them leave. Use the north exit and meet me in the courtyard. Trust me.

Rashid

Olivia took a white towel from the brass hook by the sink and opened it onto the top of the toilet tank. Then she took a lipstick from the medicine cabinet and wrote the word YES in large letters on the towel. She folded the towel and took it to Mina. "I'd appreciate it if you'd take this to the laundry man for me."

"Yes, of course, khanoum."

When Mina had gone, Olivia closed the door and glanced around the room, trying to decide what to take. Lack of sleep and the stress of the last twenty-four hours made it difficult to focus. Rashid was safe. He would help her. Just a short while longer and she'd be with him.

She went back into the bathroom and read the note again. Then she tore it into small pieces and flushed it down the toilet. She had to get ready! On her way to the dresser she remembered: she had money. She reached under the dresser, afraid it might be gone, but it was there, a thick roll wedged into a crevice between the slats: seven thousand dollars in hundred dollar bills. Karen had given it to her a few days before she died.

"You may need this someday," Karen had said. "Take care of yourself. Take care of our baby."

The wad of bills was Karen's blessing on her decision to leave. Karen's voice came to her from heaven. *Run.*

When she stuffed the bills into her pocket, Abu-Khan's ring caught on the edge of the fabric, cutting into her flesh. She wanted to throw it across the room, but it might turn out to be useful. If she was caught trying to escape, she would tell Abu-Khan she'd been planning to return as soon as the danger was past. If he saw she was still wearing the ring, he might believe she was loyal.

Abu-Khan wanted to *marry* her. She shuddered. She could never come back, not now that she knew his intentions. Hopefully seven thousand dollars and the help of a friend would buy her enough time to come up with a plan for her life.

She put clothes for Jamal and a few diapers into a diaper bag and threw it over her shoulder. Her beloved *dotar*—the stringed instrument Nur had given her— leaned against the dresser. It would be crazy to try to take it. But it would be one more loss, *one loss too many*, if she left it. She grabbed it and slung it by its strap across her back.

Jamal and the puppy were wrestling on the floor in the middle of the room. The puppy was tugging at Jamal's pant leg, and Jamal was kicking and squealing, trying to free himself. What would happen to the puppy? Probably one of the servants would throw him out onto the street, where he would eventually starve to death. If she'd had more time she could have found someone from her school to take him. One of the American or British families would have loved him. But there hadn't been time, and she couldn't worry about him now. She had to concentrate on getting out of the palace, on getting to Rashid.

Sounds in the hallway interrupted her thoughts—first shouting, then the muffled thunk of boots running across the thick carpet. There was more shouting and then…silence.

Was this it? Was it time to run? Less than ten minutes had passed since Mina brought the note. She stood listening for a moment and then opened the door and looked into the hallway. It was deserted.

The door of Jamal's room opened, and Nargess peered timidly out. "What's happening?" the girl asked.

"I'm not sure, but I know there's danger. Go, Nargess. I'll take care of Jamal. Get out of the palace as quickly as you can. Go to the kitchen. Tell the other servants to leave too."

The girl came to stand before Olivia. "But what about you? What about Jamal?"

"Don't worry. Rashid is helping us. Don't come back to the palace unless I send for you." What would happen to the girl? With Jamal gone there would be no job for her. Olivia pulled the wad of money from her pocket, peeled away four hundred-dollar bills and pressed them into the girl's hand. "Take this. May Allah bless you. Thank you."

The girl looked at the bills, her eyes round with wonder. "Yes, khanoum. Thank you, khanoum." She ran down the hallway, her chador flying behind her like a cape.

Olivia picked up Jamal, ignoring the puppy, and settled him on her hip; then she threw her chador over her head, pulling it aside so the boy could see out. "We're going for a little walk."

Jamal curled down his lips, a sure sign that tears would soon follow. "Puppy!" he wailed.

"I'm sorry, honey, the puppy can't come with us."

Jamal began sobbing in earnest, and the puppy looked up at her with soulful pleading in his eyes. Damn. No. She had to hurry. She couldn't take him.

But she couldn't leave him either.

"Oh, all right." She picked up the puppy and tucked him between herself and Jamal. "You have to hold onto him," she said to Jamal. She grabbed the worm pill from the top of her dresser and stuffed it into a pocket; then she hurried through the door into the hall.

"Puppy," Jamal purred. He wrapped his chubby little arm around the puppy's body while he clung to Olivia's neck with his other arm.

She hurried toward the servants' stairwell and then started cautiously down the narrow steps. A tall soldier stood with his back to her on the second-floor landing. She descended silently, waiting for him to notice her, hoping that as a mere woman she might not be worth his attention. The soldiers were in the palace because of the rebellion, not because of her. Abu-Khan couldn't have told the entire Behruzi army to watch for her escape!

She was only a few steps from the soldier when he saw her. He was young, perhaps no more than sixteen, and he looked frightened. "Who are you? Where are you going?"

A group of officers stood in a circle in the hall leading from the landing toward Abu-Khan's office. General Arjangi, the general who'd escorted her back to the palace the day before, was among them. Olivia turned away to hide her face from the officers and whispered to the young soldier, "I am the sultan's sister-in-law. The sultan has told me to leave. I am to tell no one."

"Oh." He started to move to the side but then hesitated. She saw Rashid on the first floor landing, signaling for her to hurry.

"Wait!" The command came from the group of officers. General Arjangi strode toward her. Nur had come out of Abu-Khan's office into the hallway.

Olivia stood frozen in indecision. Could Nur help? Would he? Could she outrun the soldiers? Could she talk her way past them?

An explosion boomed from somewhere beyond Abu-Khan's office. The general stopped and turned back toward the sound. Olivia didn't wait to see what happened. She started down the stairs toward Rashid.

"Hurry!" He was climbing the stairs toward her. There was another explosion, this time closer.

The splintering roar stunned her; then something struck her head and there was a sharp pain on her back above the place where Jamal's leg curled around her.

"Rashid!" She took another step toward him. His

arms came around her as a curtain closed over her vision. Nur called her name, and one of the soldiers screamed.

"Livie." Rashid's voice was muffled; she strained to hear it. Where was he? She drifted toward blackness.

****

"Come on, sweetheart, hang on." That was Rashid's litany, his prayer, as the car inched along through the congestion of Karush Street.

Reza and his wife Abia were talking quietly in the front seat, and Abia was reassuring Jamal, who was in her lap, but Rashid didn't join the conversation. He never took his eyes from the beloved form that lay sprawled across his lap. Olivia's head rested in the crook of his arm, and blood from an injury on her back oozed into the fabric of his sleeve.

Reza turned the car onto a quiet street near his home. "We're almost there," he said.

"We're almost there," Rashid repeated to Olivia. He gazed at her closed eyes, praying for them to open.

Rashid waited in the car while Reza rang the bell at the doctor's gate. Then he carried Olivia inside. A servant led them to the doctor's consulting room, which was beside his house, and then went to get the doctor. Rashid laid Olivia on the examining table. Her eyes twitched and then opened.

Thank God.

She licked her lips. She peered around the room, full of confusion. "Are you hurt?" she asked Rashid.

What? Was *he* hurt? Why would she ask that?

Oh. She'd noticed the blood on his shirt. "No. I'm fine. It's not my blood."

"Jamal?"

"He's all right. He's fine too." Reza and Abia are with him. I imagine they're getting him something to eat."

"The puppy?"

"What?" Rashid could scarcely believe his ears. She was concerned about the puppy? Relief flooded through him.

"He's okay. He's with Jamal." Rashid smiled. She was concerned about the puppy!

"You've been injured," Rashid said. "Can you tell me where it hurts?"

"I don't know." Her face twisted in concentration. "I don't feel anything."

He smoothed the hair away from her face, stroking across the top of her head, but stopped when he felt a lump. She winced.

"I'm sorry," he moaned. Then he shouted to anyone who might hear "Where's the doctor?"

He leaned over her, holding her, cherishing her, loving her, until the doctor came.

Chapter Five

Rashid sat on a folding chair in the corner of the small bedroom reading a newspaper. Trying to read a newspaper. Olivia lay on a mattress on the floor a few feet away. Bright sunlight streamed into the small bedroom, but still she slept. Her beautiful face, pale now, was serene in sleep. He read half a paragraph and then looked up again. She'd opened her eyes.

Thank God. He stepped over to the mattress. "Good morning, sleepyhead. How are you feeling?"

"Where am I? Where's Jamal?"

Rashid sat down cross-legged on the rug beside her. She was pale but alert. And she was here, with him, *away from the palace.* "We're in the northern part of the city, in the home of Reza's cousin Omar. Jamal is in the garden playing with the puppy and with Omar's grandchildren."

"I want to see him."

"Maybe later, when you're feeling better."

"I want to see him now." She sounded like the old assertive Olivia who once explored Behruz City with him.

"All right." But it wasn't really all right. Seeing Jamal might upset her.

"What is it? There's something you're not telling me."

"I'm sorry. Don't worry; he's fine. It's just

66

that…well…Reza has altered Jamal's appearance so he won't be recognized. He did a good job; the boy is quite transformed. I was afraid it might be a shock to you."

"What?"

"It's not anything permanent. His head has been shaved; that's the main thing. And he's wearing a different style of clothes."

"Oh." She smiled. "His head shaved?" That seemed to strike her as funny.

She was smiling. She would be okay.

"Yes, he looks like just another child who's had head lice. So now will you let him stay outside for a little while longer? You need to rest, and I assure you, he's fine. He's having a great time playing with his new friends."

"I wish I could see that. He's never had much chance to play with other children."

"You will see it. You'll be here for a few days."

"What happened?"

He told her she had a laceration on her back, which had been stitched, and she'd suffered a concussion. The doctor thought she'd be fine, but he wanted to observe her for a few days to be sure.

"The doctor will be back to see you again tomorrow, but in the meantime, there's a nurse here to take care of you, and Omar's wife Sarat will bring you food. They all think you're my wife, by the way, and Jamal is our son. It was the easiest explanation."

"Oh." Her face paled. She turned her head away.

Was the fantasy that was like a precious dream to him so painful for her to contemplate?

"Reza knows who you and Jamal are, but he won't tell anyone. They can probably guess your injuries have something to do with the rebellion, but they won't ask for details. Reza told them we prefer not to discuss the incident. I told them the baby's name is Jamie."

"Jamie?"

"Yes, I hope it's okay. It was the first name that came to mind."

She smiled a wistful smile. "It's perfect. My father's name was James."

Well, he'd gotten something right.

"Was my dotar damaged?"

"Dotar?"

"My *dotar*. It's a musical instrument. Kind of like a guitar, but with only two strings. Nur gave it to me."

Of course: the instrument she was carrying when she escaped the palace. He had to laugh. She was lying there with serious injuries—she could have been killed—and she was worried about a musical instrument. "It's fine. Omar said he'd keep it in a safe place. I couldn't believe it when I saw you carrying Jamal, the puppy, a diaper bag, and that huge thing. You were loaded like a nomad camel."

She smiled. "It would be hard to replace."

"So you play the dotar now?"

"Yes. Nur's brother has been teaching me."

"I see." He studied her. Talking about music had brought a little color to her cheeks. "You haven't asked about Abu-Khan."

She gasped. The slight pink of her cheeks disappeared. "Oh. Abu-Khan! He must be looking for us!"

"Don't worry. I sent a message to Nur. He'll have passed it along to Abu-Khan."

"What did you say?"

"Nur already knew you escaped during the attack, and he knew you were injured. He was there, actually. He carried Jamal, the puppy, and the dotar while I carried you and the diaper bag."

She almost smiled. "Nur carried the puppy?"

"Well, I guess it was technically Jamal who carried the puppy. Apparently it would take more than a few explosions to get him to let go of his beloved dog."

"Did you tell Abu-Khan where we are?" The urgent appeal on her face made him wonder again if she was afraid of Abu-Khan. And if she was, *why was she?*

"No. I didn't think it was a good idea. I told him you were in a safe place and were recovering nicely. I said you would return to the palace when things were back to normal. That is your plan, isn't it?"

She hesitated. Her eyes were shuttered, giving away nothing, but she nodded.

"I didn't mention that we're leaving the country. He won't want you to if he still thinks he can overcome the rebellion quickly. I think it's best to wait until we're outside Behruz to tell him. I'll help you figure out how to get a message to him when the time comes."

Relief crossed her face. "Thank you, Rashid. But how will we travel? I don't have my passport. Jamal doesn't have one either."

Rashid explained that the airport was closed, so they would be going overland to Iran. He said other Americans had already fled Behruz, and some had ended up in Tehran. The U.S. didn't have an embassy there, but the Swiss embassy and the Iranian Red Cross were helping them make arrangements to fly to Europe. Without telling any blatant lies, he managed to suggest that their status as refugees would make it possible to do all this without passports.

That seemed like enough information for her to take in now. He didn't try to explain how they were going to get across the border.

"What if Abu-Khan tries to stop us? The border guards may have pictures of us."

Of course she assumed they'd be going through the *main* border crossing, the one on the highway to Tehran. Let her think that for now. He told her not to worry. He said he'd make sure they weren't stopped at the border. "I have friends..." he said, implying they could somehow beg or bribe their way across.

She was apparently satisfied. So she trusted him a little.

"Abu-Khan wasn't hurt in the attack?" she asked.

So, she'd finally asked about Abu-Khan's welfare. "No. He wasn't even at the palace. He'd already left for the old fortress. He's there now."

"Oh. But he was going to take me and Jamal with him."

"Yes, so now we see how well he takes care of your safety. Your whole wing of the palace was destroyed, Livie. If you'd been in your room, you would surely have been killed."

"Thank goodness I got your note in time to send Nargess away. She would have been killed, and the puppy too. Abu-Khan probably meant to send for me later. I know he wanted us with him."

How could she be defending Abu-Khan's disregard for her safety? Rashid didn't hide his sarcasm when he answered, "I'm sure he did."

"What about the servants?" she asked. "Were any of them hurt?"

"No. One of the secretaries was injured, and several soldiers were killed, but none of the servants were hurt."

"Good. I'm so glad." She smiled at him, a grateful smile. She lifted her hand toward him and he took it. He touched his lips to her palm.

"Do you trust me then, Livie? Just a little?" He flattened her palm against his cheek. She swept her fingers across the stubble on his jaw and chin.

"Yes."

She gazed directly into his eyes. They were connected in the old way. For this moment at least, she trusted him. His heart swelled. He would not let her go again.

She reached up her free hand toward his face, and the jewel on her finger flashed a spark of green. The ring. He'd forgotten about that. What did it mean?

He grabbed her hand. They both stared silently at the ornate piece of jewelry. "Ah, I saw yesterday that you were wearing my grandmother's emerald. Would you care to tell me what it signifies?"

"It was your grandmother's? I didn't know it was an heirloom. Is it valuable?" She tried to pull her hand away, but he wouldn't let her.

"Did you think Abu-Khan got it as a prize in the bottom of a cereal box? Of course it's valuable. I wouldn't expect him to give it to anyone but his wife. Or his future wife."

"Oh, no," she whispered. "No. That's not what it means. No."

"Well then, why are you wearing it?"

She pulled her hand away and hid it under the sheet. She spoke slowly, apparently choosing her words carefully. "I have a certain loyalty to Abu-Khan. He was my sister's husband. He paid for all my years of boarding school after my parents died and for my college tuition, and he gave me a place to live during school vacations. Now he's letting me raise Jamal. I owe him my loyalty at least. He feels threatened, and he wants me to wear his ring as a show of support. It's a small thing to do."

"Hmm." Her explanation didn't quite add up. "I can see why you would be *grateful* to Abu-Khan. But loyalty? That would seem to require a respect I'm not sure you feel. And what about Abu-Khan? Can you explain the way he treated you at dinner last night?"

She looked at the window and then the ring. She seemed to be avoiding looking at him. "I don't know, but somehow I think that performance was for your benefit."

"Yes. I thought so too, but what was he trying to prove?"

She still studied the ring. She turned it round and round her finger. "He's a complex man. Don't ask me to explain his motives."

"So there's no connection between his little act last night and the reason you refused to see me two years ago?"

The blood drained from Olivia's face. She whispered, "Abu-Khan..." She started to sit up, but pain flashed across her face. She fell back against one arm and buried her face in her hands.

Rashid reached for her and eased her onto her back on the bed. "What is it, Livie?"

"It's nothing. I must have pulled at the stitches. Don't worry. I'm fine."

What was wrong with him? He should have waited until she was stronger. Damn. "I'm so sorry."

He called for the nurse and told Sarat to get the doctor. The nurse came and took Rashid's place by the bed so she could check Olivia's temperature and blood pressure and change the dressing on her wound. By the time she'd finished, the doctor had arrived.

"I'll check her out," the doctor told Rashid, but I'm sure she's fine. She needs rest. She shouldn't be excited or stressed."

Rashid felt like a boy who'd been reprimanded in school. And he deserved it. "Right. I understand." He looked at his watch. He was late for a meeting. Damn, he was always late for a meeting. "I have to leave." He touched her cheek. It was cool and soft. He kissed her quickly on the forehead and left.

He went to the corner to wait for a taxi. The last words from her lips before she hurt herself had been Abu-Khan's name. *What had she been about to say?* What was her relationship with the man? She hadn't seemed very concerned about what happened to him during the attack on the palace. She'd asked about Jamal and the puppy as soon as she regained consciousness, but she hadn't asked about Abu-Khan until Rashid reminded her. Even then she'd shown more concern for the servants' welfare.

She'd reacted with thinly veiled distaste to Abu-Khan's attentions at dinner, but now she was talking about loyalty to him? It didn't make sense. Rashid remembered wondering, when he found her with the puppy, if she could actually be *afraid* of Abu-Khan. At the time it hadn't seemed possible, but now he wondered. Did she think she had to stay in Abu-Khan's good graces because Abu-Khan controlled her access to Jamal? Surely Abu-Khan was grateful to have his son cared for by someone who so obviously loved the child.

Impatience gnawed at Rashid as speculations surfaced and spun in his mind. Determination lengthened his stride. He turned into a small alley and approached the teashop where he was to meet Saddiq. There would be no answers to his questions today. He had to concentrate on preparing for their trip to Iran, and he had to leave Olivia alone to rest and heal. But when she was recovered, when they were on the road together heading for freedom, then he would have his answers.

The phrase "to wring the truth out of her" came to mind, and his hands tensed into fists, but then his mouth stretched into a grimacing smile and he relaxed. He would need patience, not force. She'd said she trusted him. That was a start. He would have to take it one step at a time. He would have several days with her when they traveled overland to Tehran. Several days. Together. Night and day. *Night* and day. His body came to throbbing life as he imagined what those *nights* would bring. He saw himself lying in the tent they would share. Olivia was naked in the image; she was bending over him, her long hair brushing his chest, her breasts aching toward him.

No. With longing came fear. He must not lose his heart to her again.

He stopped for a moment outside the tea shop and willed thoughts of Olivia out of his mind. The smell of fresh-baked bread and the sound of clattering dishes came to him through the open door. He stooped to enter and saw that Saddiq was already there. There was another man sitting at the table with Saddiq, probably the mechanic. Good. It was time to get to work.

****

Olivia's mind raced. She could hardly pay attention to the doctor's questions and instructions. Rashid thought *she* had abandoned *him* two years ago. What would make him think that? What? Or *who?* Abu-Khan, of course. Abu-Khan had engineered their separation. Not Rashid. How could she have failed to realize?

Her heart was nearly exploding with happiness and hope, and her mind was busy rehearsing how she would tell Rashid.

But could she tell him about Abu-Khan's manipulations without also telling him about Jamal and about Abu-Khan's threats?

What would he do if she told him everything?

He would go back to the palace to confront Abu-Khan. There would be no stopping him. She was back to her old anxiety and fear. She could never tell Rashid.

Sarat brought Jamal to Olivia's room after the doctor left. His bald head struck her as a little comical, but in a way his appearance was more natural than when his hair was black. He was wearing loose pants and a long, collarless shirt of white cotton: the type of shirt worn by nomads and men of the countryside. Rashid had been wearing a shirt like that. She'd always thought of him as being more European than Middle Eastern, but with the long shirt falling from his strong shoulders and a thick stubble darkening the shadows of his face, he'd looked like one of the proud nomads of the mountainous south.

He'd told everyone he was her husband and Jamal

was their son. It was all a necessary little fiction as far as Rashid was concerned, but for her it was a chance to live a dream for a few days. It was more than she'd dared hope for, and it would have to be enough.

She sat up and held Jamal for a while—he had a new toy truck to show her—and they ate breakfast together. Then he went out to the courtyard to play with his new friends. Olivia tried to rest, but she couldn't stop thinking about her last conversation with Rashid. Had she revealed too much? Her apparent loyalty to Abu-Khan must seem ridiculous to Rashid.

Rashid came back later in the afternoon. He had books and toiletries for her, toys and diapers for Jamal, and clothes for both of them.

He said he had her roll of hundred-dollar bills. A nurse had found it in her pocket the previous night and had given it to Rashid. "I was wondering where you got so much money. Did Abu-Khan give it to you?"

Olivia smiled a bitter smile. Abu-Khan most certainly had not given her anything that would help her feel more independent. "No. Karen gave it to me before she died. I don't know where she got it. Maybe she inherited it from my parents."

"Or maybe Abu-Khan gave it to her?" Rashid ventured.

No. He wouldn't have wanted Karen to have options any more than he wanted Olivia to have them. "I'm sure he didn't just hand it to her, but she might have accumulated it bit by bit. He gave her money whenever she had a chance to go shopping."

She liked the idea of Karen wheedling money out of Abu-Khan and saving it for some goal of her own. She hated to think Karen had been as subservient to

Abu-Khan as she always seemed.

Rashid stood up. "I have to go. I have a lot to do to get ready. Look through the things I've brought and let me know if there's anything else you need. I'll be back tomorrow evening." He bent over her, kissed her on the lips, and left.

She stared at the door after he closed it, dazed. The kiss had been so casual and so quickly over—like the everyday kiss of a married couple saying goodbye at the beginning of a workday. Like a kiss that didn't have to push for more because there would be plenty of opportunities for *more*.

Would there be opportunities for more?

Omar set up a crib next to Olivia's bed, and Sarat came into the room now and then to bring food. They must have been curious—about the busy husband who came for brief visits, about the child who dressed like a Behruzi peasant, and about the injuries they must have guessed were in some way connected to the rebellion— but the only personal question they asked was about Olivia's age.

"I don't believe it," Sarat gasped when she learned Olivia was twenty-three. "I thought you were fifteen or sixteen."

Olivia smiled. Behruzis always thought she looked young, probably because of her slender, boyish figure.

Olivia tortured herself for the rest of the day with anxiety about what she should tell Rashid. All her rehearsed little conversations ended with him storming off to confront Abu-Khan and claim his son. She practiced in her mind the arguments she would use to stop him, but they wouldn't work. He would go. He didn't know how really obsessed and dangerous Abu-

Khan was. He would go, and he would not come back.

Or he would come back in the custody of soldiers who would seize Jamal.

She could imagine creating a simple life for herself and Jamal, but she wasn't able to fit Rashid into the picture. Even if he forgave her and wanted to be with her, he couldn't live in hiding as she would have to do. Rashid had a career he loved, and he had friends and family in California.

Anyway, he would never believe it was necessary to live in hiding. He would insist on confronting Abu-Khan. It was so much in Rashid's nature to tackle problems head-on, and, in spite of their many arguments, he loved and trusted his uncle. He would be sure he could convince Abu-Khan to do "the honorable thing."

And so, in the end, after all her analyses, she knew she couldn't tell Rashid the truth. She would separate from him as soon as they got out of Behruz, and then she would never see him again.

When he came the following evening, he brought a deck of cards, and they played piquet, a game he'd taught her when she was a teenager. They wagered small change, as they'd always done, and bickered about the rules, which were complex and had dimmed in both their memories. Olivia won the first game, and Rashid paid what he owed, which was the equivalent of about a dollar.

"Again?" he asked. "Are you going to give me a chance to win my money back?"

"Yes, of course." She laughed.

She was sitting on the mattress cross-legged, and he was sitting on the rug. He smoothed the blanket they were using as a playing surface and leaned back, regarding her. "What has your life been like since Karen died?"

"Oh." She was caught off-guard. *Be careful.*

"I take care of Jamal, and I spend a few hours a day at the school. It's a simple life."

"I see. Do you play music at all?"

Music. A safe subject. "Just a little. There's a piano at school. I play it by myself sometimes, just to relax, and I play for dance recitals and the Christmas pageant and things like that."

"Dance recitals?"

"Yes." She laughed. "I teach dance, believe it or not. The American mothers begged me to. I told them I'm not qualified—I haven't studied dance since I was a kid—but they insisted, so I do the best I can."

"You're a beautiful dancer. I'm sure if you'd kept up with it you'd have had as much success in dance as you've had with your music."

She shuffled the cards and dealt them and they returned to their play, silent and intent like chess players vying for the world title.

"What about your violin?" Rashid asked when they'd finished another game. "Do you have it here?"

"No, it's in storage in Boston."

"You must miss it."

"Yes." She missed it. The violin represented all she'd given up to be with her son. "But I have my dotar."

"Oh, that's right. You said Nur's brother taught you?"

"Yes. We had our lessons in the courtyard, and sometimes we played little impromptu duets for the servants."

"I'd forgotten Nur had a brother. It's always seemed as if *we* were his family."

"He has a brother and three sisters and a slew of nieces and nephews who adore him. They all live on Ferdos Street. Don't you remember when we stuck a flag in his mail slot?"

"Oh that's right. The flags…" It had been her second summer in Behruz. She was spending the entire summer, and Rashid was there for three weeks. One day at the beginning of July a box of tiny American flags showed up at the plastic store. Rashid bought a handful and presented them to Olivia. "To my American friend for her American holiday."

Olivia shuffled the cards slowly, her mind lost in the past. "You didn't consider yourself an American, did you?"

"No, I didn't. I was still having a pretty tough time at school. That was before I joined the soccer team."

"I suppose as soon as they saw what a great soccer player you were your troubles were over."

"It wasn't quite that easy, but yes, I guess it was a turning point."

"Do you think of yourself as American now?" she asked.

"No, not really. I'm afraid I'll always be stuck between two worlds."

"Well, I am still one hundred percent American. Remember how I planted those little flags in all the flower pots we saw on our way home?"

"And in the key holes and latches of people's gates and in their mail slots."

"Then you climbed up onto that statue of the old

sultan on Darrous Street and wedged a flag into his hand!"

They both laughed. She realized she hadn't laughed like that for two years. She felt carefree.

Would he kiss her again when it was time for him to leave?

She dealt the cards with that possibility tingling on her lips.

"We'll be leaving for Iran the day after tomorrow," he said when he stood up to leave. "Can you be ready?"

She said that she could.

He bent toward her, probably about to give her another perfunctory kiss, but she got to her knees and stood up too. *Time for more.* She turned her face to him. She closed her eyes. She waited.

"You little vixen." His hands touched her cheeks and threaded into her hair. She smiled, her lips quivering in anticipation, but she kept her eyes closed.

The kiss came finally, soft and tentative at first, but definitely not a quick little smack. She put her arms around his waist and felt his heart drumming its steady beat against her breast. The kiss deepened, and his erection pressed into her belly. She shifted and writhed, wanting *more*, and his arms came around her back to pull her even more tightly into the shelter of his body.

But then, when she had lost herself in the kiss, when all she wanted in the world was for it to go on forever, he pulled away.

"You're playing with fire, little girl. I'll see you in two days." He slipped through the door and was gone.

The fire she'd been playing with still burned in her loins.

More.

Chapter Six

Two days later, Olivia awoke to the sound of Rashid's voice. She saw him when she came out of her room, standing across the large foyer from her, leaning against the jamb of the kitchen doorway. Sarat was at the sink, and Omar was sitting at the table drinking tea. The three of them were talking and laughing.

Olivia moved quietly because Jamal was still asleep. Rashid hadn't heard her open the door, and he didn't see her gazing at him.

He looked like an image from the pages of one of her American mail-order catalogs in that pose. He was clean-shaven now and was wearing a dark suit and white shirt with no tie. The jacket sleeves were pushed up to expose his muscular forearms, and the shirt was open at the collar. Strength and power emanated from him.

He turned toward her before she had a chance to collect herself, before she had a chance to erect her defenses. He straightened when he saw her. Olivia's body quivered in response to the power of him, and she felt as exposed as if she'd been standing there naked. She was wearing clothes he'd brought her: American jeans, a cotton knit sweater from Italy, and lacy underpants from France. But no bra. The one she'd been wearing had been thrown away when the doctor stitched her, and Rashid hadn't brought one. It hadn't seemed important while she was staying here. Sarat, with her melon-sized breasts, didn't even wear one. But now, with Rashid's eyes on her, she felt conscious of the lines of her body. She was aware of the soft cotton of the sweater on her breasts, and liquid heat stirred through her legs.

She couldn't collect herself, couldn't restrain her response to him. She just stood there. Waiting.

"You're thin," he said in Farsi.

"I know," Sarat said from the kitchen. "I've tried to get her to eat more. I've tried to fix things she likes."

Rashid stepped across the marble floor to stand facing Olivia. He gripped her shoulders and looked down at her with a possessive gleam in his eyes. "Hello wife," he said in Farsi. He laced his fingers into her hair, cradling her head, and gave her a kiss that said he too was impatient for *more*. This kiss said the time for *more* was approaching. He lifted his head, ending the kiss, but his hands still sheltered her head.

"So then, you've missed me just a little?" He spoke in English now.

"Oh," Olivia moaned. Embarrassment flooded her cheeks. Sarat and Omar were watching from the kitchen, smiling.

She backed away, groping for the doorknob behind her, but Rashid stepped toward her, reached around her to open the door, and moved her with his body into the bedroom.

"You shouldn't have done that," she whispered. He closed the door.

"Shouldn't have done what?"

"You shouldn't have kissed me. Omar and Sarat wouldn't expect it. I don't think a Behruzi couple would ever make such a display in front of other people."

"You're right, they wouldn't, but I'm sure Omar and Sarat have seen enough American television to give them ideas about Western ways. I didn't want to disappoint them."

"You shouldn't have done it, and you shouldn't be in here now. What will they think?"

"They'll think I'm happy to see my wife, which happens to be true."

"Don't tease me, Rashid. Please." He took her into his arms and kissed her again. His kiss was hungry, and her response was hungry too. She threw her arms around his neck; she pressed against him. She wanted more.

He was the one to end it. His kisses grew lighter, and he moved his hands up to tilt her head back. He kissed her again, one last time, lips closed, firmly, *decisively*, and he stepped away. "You'd better get ready. We have a long trip ahead of us." He left the room and closed the door.

She slumped onto the mattress and lay waiting for her thudding pulse to subside. Jamal was awake. He was sitting in the crib, his eyes wide and curious, apparently having observed the scene with Rashid.

She picked him up and hugged him. He melted against her, all baby softness, but after a while he squirmed to get free. "Let's hope this is a quick trip." She laid him on the bed and prepared to change his diaper. She didn't think her nerves could take much more of having Rashid toy with her emotions. Could they make it to Tehran today? She doubted it. Where would they stay if they had to stop for the night? Would

Rashid expect to share a room? And what would she say if he did? An image came to her mind of them in a hotel room in some unknown town in Iran. Jamal was asleep. Rashid's mouth was plundering hers as it had a few minutes ago. There was a bed nearby…

She shook the image out of her mind. She mustn't allow herself to think like that. Rashid was right when he said she was playing with fire. She couldn't share her body with him without opening her heart as well, and there would be no holding back her secrets if she did that.

****

Rashid gripped the steering wheel and pulled at it in a surge of nervous triumph. Olivia sat beside him, camouflaged by her chador, looking at the sights of the city. They'd made it. She was here with him and they were on their way. There could be dangers yet to face, but the hard part—getting her to agree to come, getting her out of the palace, waiting for her to get well—was behind him.

He reviewed in his mind the challenges that lay ahead. The first part, the drive to the mountains was the most risky. Abu-Khan's soldiers were probably watching for them. There could be roadblocks. After they got off the road, when they were trekking through the mountains, they should be safe from soldiers, but then Olivia's stamina would be a factor. Was she strong enough? He wasn't too worried about the actual border. Hopefully their disguises would get them past any soldiers they found there. That would be the final hurdle. Once they crossed into Iran, they would be free.

The greatest danger of all was the woman beside him. With her silky hair and urchin eyes; with her long, slender limbs and her way of moving as if life was a dance. Livie with her secrets. He hadn't meant to kiss her—he had so much to lose if he didn't keep a strict rein on his feelings—but he'd been so glad to finally be on the road, and something about her expression had been so inviting.

It was dangerous to think about a possible future with her, but he couldn't stop his mind from weaving hopes and speculations. Maybe this time things would be different. If only she would explain what went wrong two years ago. If only she would tell him what she was afraid of now. His grip on the steering wheel tightened. He'd been so insistent that she trust him, but was there anything she could say—after abandoning him two years ago—that would ever make *him* trust *her* again?

There were army jeeps and foot soldiers at every corner, but the shops were open and there was the usual bustle of activity on the sidewalks.

"This is a nice car," she said.

Rashid laughed. "Actually, it's an Iranian-built Paykan, which is about the cheapest car ever made, and it's about twenty years old. Didn't you notice the dents?"

"Yes, but the engine is so quiet. It sounds like one of the expensive cars of Abu-Khan's fleet. And the seats are so comfortable."

"I chose a Paykan because I thought a fancier car might attract attention. But I had some work done on it." Actually he'd spent thousands of dollars getting the car ready for the trip. But she didn't need to know that.

They drove out of the business district into the southern part of the city, past houses made of crumbling mud bricks. Barefoot children played in the ditches that brought water to their homes.

"I've never seen this part of the city," she said. "Are these the people who are fighting Abu-Khan?"

"Not exactly. I imagine these people are too busy just trying to survive. Still, the most idealistic among the rebels do talk about improving conditions for the poor."

"Do they want more freedom for women?"

Of course she would think of the women. "That will take time, Livie. There is no one to speak for the women. Not yet."

She asked questions about the rebellion, and he told her what he knew.

"It's hard for me to take in," she said. "Abu-Khan never told me anything about it, not until you arrived."

She must have been practically a prisoner in the palace to have been so shielded from what was going on. How could his smart, assertive Livie have accepted such a restricted life?

How could he have left her to that life for so long?

"Abu-Khan was foolish to think this threat would just go away. He should have left the palace weeks ago." He should have gotten *her* out of the palace. And Jamal. "He thinks he's invincible, but he's not. I've met with the leaders; I saw their resolve. They won't give up until they see change."

"You were with them that morning at the meeting, the one that was supposed to take place at the university, weren't you? I was so afraid Abu-Khan would learn of the new location."

"The meeting was held in the back of a produce store owned by one of the leaders. I didn't stay long. I could tell pretty quickly it was too late for mediation. One of the students told me about the planned attack on the palace, and I left immediately." Rashid had been afraid that morning too. He'd been afraid he wouldn't get to the palace in time. And he'd been afraid Olivia might refuse to go with him.

"Who would take power if Abu-Khan were to be overthrown?"

"I don't know. I suppose it would be someone from the military, but it might be a religious leader. That's what happened in Iran. Behruzis have no experience in *choosing* a leader, so there's no system in place. It could be anyone who's strong enough to seize power."

"How will this affect Jamal? Do you think there's a chance he'll be able to escape his so-called 'destiny' as the future sultan?"

He'd never thought about how a revolution would affect Jamal's future, but of course she had. There were complexities in her situation that had never occurred to him. "It's hard to tell; there are so many unknowns. The next few weeks will reveal a lot."

"What about you, Rashid? Is there any circumstance that would put you in line to be sultan?"

He laughed. "No, thank God. My father was actually Abu-Khan's *half*-brother. They have different fathers. I don't have a drop of royal blood in me."

"Oh!" She sat forward and turned toward him. "I didn't know your fathers were *half* brothers. Why that changes everything, doesn't it?"

He laughed again. She seemed awfully pleased to find out he was *not* in line for royal duty. "Well, it doesn't change anything for me. I've always known I was a commoner."

She sat back and they rode in silence. They passed a match factory and a bicycle assembly plant, and then they were on a two-lane highway through a barren plain with jagged mountains in the distance. There was very little traffic, just an occasional army jeep. The few villages they saw were all some distance off the highway. The buildings, which were made of local clay, blended in with the landscape.

"You can pull your chador away from your face," Rashid said. "Just keep your hair covered."

Olivia did as he suggested. A wisp of her silken hair fell free, and he reached to tuck it under the edge of the fabric. When his knuckles grazed her cheek, she slanted her face into his touch and electricity jolted between them. He cupped her cheek, and let his hand brush down the side of her face before returning it to the steering wheel.

She said nothing, but the air was charged with unspoken questions, unspoken feelings, and memories of the kisses they'd shared that morning. Rashid shifted uncomfortably in the seat. The memory of those kisses was too fresh, too raw. His body's yearnings had not been satisfied. Was Olivia's body still clamoring for more?

Jamal was asleep in a car seat behind them, his head drooped to the side, his arm in a stranglehold around the neck of the puppy, who was also asleep. Rashid felt a protective tenderness for all three of them, the woman, the baby, and the puppy. If only the lie he'd told Omar were the truth. If only they really were a family. Father and mother—husband and wife—with their baby and the family pet on a family outing, maybe going away for the weekend. He saw it. He felt it. He wanted it.

He shook himself. He couldn't afford to want *that*. "Does he always sleep in the car?"

"He's never been in a car before, not since he was a few weeks old, except when you took him to Reza's. This is all new for him."

"Oh, I see." Rashid glanced at her and then returned his eyes to the road. If Jamal's life had been that restricted, then no doubt hers had been too.

Jamal woke a few minutes later and grew restless.

"I brought a few toys for him," Rashid said. "They're in the bag at your feet."

The toys amused him for a while, but soon he was whining and squirming against the constraints of the car seat. Rashid started to watch for a place to stop. When he spotted a cluster of poplar trees and a few bushes not far from the highway, he drove down a bumpy slope and parked the car in the shade of one of the trees.

As soon as Rashid opened the door, the puppy bounded out of the car and ran from tree to tree, sniffing frantically. Rashid freed Jamal from the straps of the car seat and then opened Olivia's door. They stood for a moment enjoying the cool mountain air. The vacant flatness of the surrounding land made the little oasis seem like a charmed place.

"We'll be coming to a town soon, and I'll stop at a gas station to ask about the road ahead. The bathroom will probably be filthy, if they even have one, so you might want to take advantage of the bit of privacy you can find behind one of those bushes."

While she did as Rashid suggested, he set up a basin of water for washing and laid a rug in the shade of one of the trees. Olivia changed Jamal's diaper and washed her face and hands; then she sat down on the rug and watched Rashid carry food from the car and set up a camp stove.

"I'm amazed at all the planning that went into this trip," she said.

He felt proud. And he felt exposed. His need to protect her and make her comfortable were screaming evidence of how he felt.

He'd brought chicken salad with raisins and pistachios, flat bread, and a green Persian melon.

"I didn't realize how hungry I was," Olivia said. "Everything looks delicious."

Rashid sat down beside her and sliced the melon. When Olivia called to Jamal to join them, the boy picked up the puppy and started the slow tottering walk to the rug. They watched, both holding their breath when he seemed about to fall.

"Should I help him?" Rashid asked.

"No, he can manage. This is good for him. He was slow to walk, and he still prefers to crawl, but there's no way he can crawl while he's hanging onto that puppy. Don't worry; he can do it."

A few steps later, he did fall, landing on his well-padded bottom. His efforts to get back up without dropping the puppy were so comical they laughed. They were friends again, for at least a moment, friends in the old way—before there was passion and rejection, before there were secrets. This was the Olivia he'd fallen in love with two years ago.

When Jamal reached them, he dropped the puppy onto the rug and sat down next to Rashid. The puppy made a leap for the chicken salad, but Rashid grabbed him and carried him to the car. There he gave him a bone. The puppy attacked it with aggressive growls and excited little yips while Olivia served the food and they ate.

"I can't believe you brought a bone for the puppy," Olivia said.

Rashid handed her a cup of tea he'd made on the camp stove. "I couldn't believe you had the puppy with you when you were leaving the palace. I never knew you were a dog lover."

"I'm not, really. It was Jamal who insisted on bringing him. The two of them sort of ganged up on me."

Jamal was busy eating the raisins out of what remained of the chicken salad. When he finished, he toddled to the car and plopped down in the dust to watch the puppy's attack on the bone. Olivia sipped her tea and leaned back against one arm, allowing the chador to fall away from her body. A light breeze rustled the poplar leaves and wafted through her hair.

Rashid stretched out on his back with his arms folded under his head, lazy and glutted with food and happiness. Olivia smiled at him. "That was a very nice meal. Thank you."

"You're welcome. I'm glad you enjoyed it. I'm happy to see you relax. You look very beautiful right now with the wind in your hair and..." His eyes scanned her slender body. "And with a little bloom back in your cheeks."

She stiffened and pulled the chador across her breast. "Shouldn't we be leaving? Can we reach Tehran today?"

"Yes, we should be going." He ignored her question about Tehran. He would have to explain his plan soon. But not yet. He stood up and offered her a hand.

Pain flashed across her face when he started to pull.

Rashid brought his hands to her sides to steady her and uttered a swear word in Farsi. "Are you all right?"

"Yes, I'm fine. I think I just stretched the skin where I was stitched." Their eyes met, and it was as it had been that morning. The air grew thicker, charged with desire. She swayed toward him. His hands, which had been flattened against her rib cage, moved of their own volition—up until his thumbs touched the swell of her breasts, down along her ribs and hips to the tops of her thighs, and then up again. Each time the sweep of his hands reached her breasts he claimed more until at last he took them into his hands. A low moan came like a purr from Olivia's throat, and her arms rose to encircle his neck. She parted her lips. She was open and inviting and *his*. He wrapped his arms around her and pulled her to him. His lips moved across hers. Their tongues touched; she pressed against him. His hands slid up and down her back, gentle over the place where she'd been hurt but hard and demanding along the small of her back. With his hands on her buttocks, he pulled her against his throbbing groin.

The sound of a passing car penetrated Rashid's lust-glazed consciousness. He should stop. He had to stop.

He released her mouth and pressed a solemn kiss between her brows. He whispered into her hair at her temple, "You are still mine, Livie."

"No." Her body went stiff. "No, I'm not. I can't be."

"Why, Livie?" *Why why why? Just tell me!*

She didn't answer, but now he knew one thing: *she remembered.* She remembered and she still had feelings for him. She was fighting those feelings because of something she feared, something to do with Abu-Khan and Jamal.

"What happened?" he asked. "Why did you leave me two years ago? How could you leave after the night we shared, after all we meant to each other?" He should let it go—he knew he needed to be patient—but he couldn't. "Have you forgotten what it was like to lie in my arms, to be kissed, to be worshipped, in every secret part of you? Have you forgotten the feelings that made you moan and whimper and cry out my name with that innocent eagerness of yours?"

"Please, Rashid," she moaned. "It was a long time ago. Everything has changed. We've changed. Can't you just let it go?"

Let it go? Really? "I can't, Livie. I've tried but I can't, and I won't let you, not any more. Every time I touch you, you remember. I know you do. I don't know what you're afraid of, but I'm going to find out."

She was trembling. He raised his hands to her shoulders. Her eyes glistened with unshed tears. He looked into those sad, beloved green eyes and silently vowed, *I will find out.* He would earn her trust and learn her secrets and solve whatever problem she had. He would win her love. It would take several days to cross the mountains. Several days of twenty-four-hour-a-day intimacy. Right now, the important thing was to get off this highway. Once they were in the mountains, he could relax and focus his attention on learning what he wanted to know.

She was quiet while they prepared to leave and while they drove to the village. He stopped at a gas station, which was, as expected, a filthy place with no amenities. The only spot of color in the whole drab setting was a beat-up Coca Cola cooler. Rashid bought two bottles of Coke, which were, miraculously, ice cold, and took one to Olivia where she stood waiting by the car.

The attendant walked with him back to the car. "Where are you headed?" he asked Rashid. Olivia must have noticed the man's accent, which was characteristic of southern Behruz, for she was suddenly all attention. She glanced at the sun and then, suspiciously, at Rashid. She must have realized they were heading south, not west toward Tehran.

So the time had come. When they were back on the road, he would explain his plan.

"We're going to Bandar-i-Shar to see my parents," he told the worker. "How's the road ahead?"

"The road is fine, but there's been fighting in Gemdar, and soldiers have put up a roadblock on this side of the town."

Olivia got back in the car and opened the glove compartment. She'd found a map and was studying it when Rashid slipped back into the driver's seat.

"Where the hell are we going?" she asked in the stern monotone she used when she wanted Jamal's attention.

He smiled. "I don't remember you talking like that before."

"Where are you taking me?"

"I've been meaning to tell you about that, but I didn't want to worry you."

She put the map back in the glove compartment. "Well, you are worrying me."

He started the engine and pulled onto the road. "We can't take the main road to Tehran. There are roadblocks all along it, and the border officials are sure to be watching for us. So we're crossing at a point a little to the south."

"I thought there was only one crossing over the border to Iran."

"There's only one *official* crossing. See that snow-capped mountain on the right? That's Gemdar Kuh. There's a pass that crosses the border just south of the mountain. The nomads use it during their migration; they've used it for centuries. Abu-Khan's father and the old shah of Iran both tried to force them to stay in their own countries, but it was like trying to hold back a force of nature. So, although it's officially illegal, the nomads still go back and forth between Behruz and Iran on their ancient trails."

"Can you drive through the pass?" Olivia asked.

"No." Rashid studied her, gauging her strength and her resolve. Was she up to the travel ahead? Would she see that this was their only option? "We'll cross on horseback with my friend Saddiq, who's a member of the Qashami tribe. We'll travel with his family."

Excitement gleamed in her eyes, and his heart responded with a leap of anticipation. "How long will it take?" she asked.

"Four or five days, maybe a week. Once we get off the highway, we'll take our time. I don't want to strain you; I know you're not fully recovered. I would have left you at Omar's longer, but it was only a matter of time before the military put up roadblocks along here. It wasn't safe to wait any longer."

"What about the roadblock at Gemdar, the one the man at the gas station told you about?"

"We'll turn off before we get to it."

And once they were off the highway, he'd feel safe. Olivia couldn't turn back then, and Abu-Khan's soldiers couldn't find them. He would learn the secrets that made Olivia deny her feelings.

He had to.

Chapter Seven

Four or five days. Maybe a week. Traveling with nomads. Through the mountains. With Rashid! Exhilaration coursed through Olivia. It would take longer than she'd expected to reach Tehran.

She looked at the long ridge of mountains that ran parallel to the highway. Which gap in those mountains was the pass they would take? What would the trek be like? *Where would they sleep?* She pictured herself standing in a high mountain meadow like Julie Andrews in The Sound of Music, her arms outstretched, spinning and singing with joy. She saw herself stretched out in a nomad tent, *in Rashid's arms.*

The sky was immense and dazzling blue. It made her feel small. And she wanted to feel small. She wanted to be a tiny, inconsequential speck of humanity who could pass unnoticed through those mountains and could board a plane in Tehran unnoticed and could lead a simple life in New England without attracting attention.

She wasn't used to wide vistas, and she wasn't used to hope, but suddenly she felt the possibility of true freedom, and her heart opened up.

She couldn't imagine Rashid leading a small life with her. She couldn't hope for that much. But *four or five days, maybe a week!* Those days stretched before her big and open like the sky, and made her blood thrum with anticipation.

What would the sleeping arrangements be once they joined the nomads?

She found herself watching the road, trying to see if there was a roadblock in the distance, waiting when they met another car to see if it was an army jeep. She saw a few, but they just sped past, and Rashid seemed confident as he navigated the narrow highway. Only when he looked at Olivia did the shadow of worry cross his face.

"Can't you relax?" he asked after a while. "It's going to be a long day; I don't want you to tire yourself. I'd planned to spend the night at the hotel in Gemdar and then come back to the turnoff, but that won't be possible now because of the roadblock. I'm afraid we'll have to push on all the way to the nomad camp. Please try to rest."

Rashid's concern and the tenderness in his voice made her feel weak. Tears threatened for no reason, and a heavy pain pushed up in her chest. She'd yearned for some sign of his caring for two lonely years, and now her heart grabbed at every scrap of it he offered.

"Come here." Rashid put his arm around her shoulders, pulling her to him.

She slid closer and allowed him to nudge her head down onto his shoulder. She closed her eyes and nestled against him, embarrassed by her need but unable to resist. There was such comfort in being near him, in the touch of his hand where it cradled her head, in the strength of the hard muscles where her cheek rested on his shoulder. Did she remember? he'd asked.

Oh yes. She'd relived that night of passion in her mind many times, but his apparent rejection of her afterward had always soured her memories. She'd felt she was a fool to have believed he might actually love her.

But now that she knew he hadn't abandoned her, the memories came back unclouded by bitterness.

She remembered how excited she'd been that he was coming. She'd gone backpacking in Europe instead of coming to Behruz the previous summer, so it had been two years since she'd seen him. They would have a lot to talk about. She would tell him about the concerts she'd given that spring, about her trip to Europe, and about her plans for Juilliard...and he would tell her about his engagement.

She'd seen pictures of Rashid's girlfriend Shamsi, a beautiful Behruzi woman who lived in California, and she'd heard about her from Abu-Khan, who was wildly enthusiastic about the match, but she still had many questions for Rashid. She didn't know how he and Shamsi had met, when the wedding would take place, how Rashid felt. All Abu-Khan cared about was that Shamsi was from an important family in Behruz, and the marriage was going to be politically advantageous to him.

On the afternoon he was expected to arrive, she sat on a bench in the courtyard reading—or trying to read—and waiting. It seemed like forever, but it had probably been only about an hour when he finally arrived. She looked up, and there he was, about twenty feet away, gazing at her with an expression she'd never seen on his face, an expression that fired neurons in her body that had never come to life before.

She could barely breathe. Everything changed in an instant. Challenges were laid down. Promises were made. Their hearts connected. No words were needed.

The words they did exchange were irrelevant and stilted. How was his trip? Was he tired? Hungry?

He sat on the bench with her, his suitcase at his feet. They stared at the grass before them. The stilted conversation about his state of fatigue and hunger became a stilted conversation about her life—about the concerts, the trip, and her plans for the following year. He told her about his work.

And then Olivia blurted that she'd heard he was engaged.

"Oh, yes, Shamsi…"

Then they were silent. Olivia continued to study the grass.

"What about you?" Rashid asked after a while. "Are you still seeing what's-his-name?"

"Bryan."

"Right. Are you still seeing Bryan?"

"No. He's going to Stanford for graduate school, and I'll be at Juilliard, so it got complicated." She plucked a thick blade of grass and stretched it between her thumbs. "He wanted me to go to California with him, but I couldn't, and I didn't think a long-distance relationship would work, so I ended it."

"You don't appear to be heartbroken."

Being reminded of Bryan brought nostalgia and a shred of regret, but mostly it brought relief. She blew through the blade of grass, making a whistling sound. "No, I'm fine. It was time to end it."

Rashid plucked a blade and twirled it between his fingers. "You sound about the same as you did after you broke up with that senior you were going with during your sophomore year."

"That was another romance that became geographically unfeasible."

She whistled through the grass again; her heart thumped slow and loud in her chest.

Rashid. Oh but of course. Why hadn't she realized?

Nur came out to say Abu-Khan was waiting for Rashid inside. They rose and walked into the palace together.

She wasn't alone with him for the rest of the day— or the day after that. Karen and Abu-Khan were intent on including their young relatives in all the official dinners and functions of the palace.

She lay in bed at night burning with desire, wanting to be in his arms but not knowing what to do. They were on the same floor of the palace. He was in the south wing, and she was in the north wing. Could she just walk down the corridor and knock on his door? It would be so brazen. He was *engaged.* She couldn't muster the courage.

At lunch on the third day Rashid suggested they go for a walk after they finished eating.

"But I'm meeting with my generals this afternoon," Abu-Khan said. "I wanted you to be at the meeting with me."

"It will be hot," Karen added. "You shouldn't go out during the heat of the day."

Olivia stifled a laugh. The idea that a room full of generals or a little heat would stop them from being together seemed like the funniest of jokes. She said, "Yes, I'd love to go for a walk."

She wore her chador, but he took her hand through the thin cloth as soon as they were on the street. They smiled at each other like conspirators. Like lovers.

"Where should we go?" Rashid asked.

They couldn't think of a single place in the entire city where they could be alone.

They walked with no particular destination in mind, their hands clasped, frustrations and anticipation zinging through the cloth that separated them. After some meandering, old habits led them to Reza's pharmacy.

Reza greeted Rashid with a hug and the usual ritual kisses on the cheek. "Hello. How are you? Is this your little American friend all grown up?"

"Yes, this is the sultan's sister-in-law, Olivia."

Reza told them about his son who had just entered the university, and Rashid told the older man about his work. When they'd caught up on their news, Rashid said, "Olivia and I haven't seen each other for two years, and we have some things we need to discuss. Is there somewhere around here where we could talk privately for a few minutes?"

"Hmm, I see. Yes." Reza's eyes followed the movement as Rashid took Olivia's hand. He smiled. "My children are at school, and my wife is at her sister's. Why don't you go into the garden? You won't be disturbed there."

And so they found themselves sitting on a bench behind a hedge of heavily scented roses, facing a vine-covered wall. Alone.

Rashid eased the chador away from her face and let it drop to her shoulders. His hands shook against her cheek when he grasped the edge of the fabric.

He drew her to him. He kissed her, a sliding, merging, urging, wet kiss that went on and on. Her mouth opened; she tasted him. She pressed against him.

His hands reached under the chador. Then under her clothes. Then under her bra. She shifted over onto his lap. She felt his hardness thrusting up toward her. She rocked against it. She wanted him. It was Rashid. It was crazy. She wanted him, his body, his hardness. She couldn't think about anything else but wanting wanting wanting…Rashid.

"This is ridiculous," he said. "We're acting like teenagers." They laughed and kissed again while Rashid's hands skimmed across her breasts. It was agony. It was bliss.

Reza's children arrived home. Their voices came through the rose hedge, calling to Rashid.

He whispered into her ear, "Come to my room tonight."

"Yes," she answered. She returned to the seat beside him. She pulled her chador back over her head.

Yes.

Dinner that night was served in the smaller of the two formal dining rooms at a table long enough to seat twenty. The guest list consisted of a general with his wife, the Minister of Health with his wife, two ambassadors with their wives, one of Abu-Khan's aunts with her husband, and a Behruzi actress who'd just finished a role in an American movie.

Abu-Khan had a lively discussion with the actress about how they might get an American film company to make a movie in Behruz.

Olivia sat next to the general's wife, a university math professor who had traveled widely and had studied in the U.S. The woman was interesting, but Olivia had a hard time concentrating on the conversation.

Across the table from her, Rashid sat talking in English to the ambassador from Egypt. The conversation was mostly about the ambassador's grandson, who was a soccer player. Rashid seemed to be trying to ignore Olivia's presence, and she was trying too, but their eyes kept meeting. The intensity of his gaze, the longing there, made her look quickly away, at her plate or at the professor. At one point, the situation struck her as so crazy and nerve-wracking and exciting, she burst into uneasy giggles. Rashid laughed too, and all conversation ceased while everyone's attention turned to them.

They stopped laughing. Olivia reached for her water goblet and took a sip, but her attempt to stifle one more eruption of laughter made the water go down her windpipe. She coughed and sputtered, while the math professor patted her on the back.

Rashid's face was red. He was struggling to hold in his laughter.

"What is the matter?" Abu-Khan asked, somehow implying that Olivia was willfully disrupting his dinner party.

"Nothing. I'm sorry. I'm fine," Olivia kept her eyes on her plate, knowing that another glimpse of Rashid's face would have her laughing again. She asked to be excused as soon as she finished her pastry.

Abu-Khan said for all to hear, "Yes, if you must. I imagine you're still recovering from your fit." He made her "fit" sound like a child's tantrum.

She waited for an hour, impatiently pacing her room, before she donned her chador and crept along the empty corridors to Rashid's room. His door was partly ajar. It swung open when she pushed, and she stepped inside. Rashid stood in the middle of the room.

Waiting for her.

She went into his arms. They embraced and kissed, a long, deep, shattering kiss, and then they reached impatiently for buttons and zippers, each other's and their own, in a frenzy of need.

Rashid used protection the first time, which was a whirlwind so intense it was quickly over, and the second time, which was slower, with more time for exploring and touching and sighing and laughing.

But not the third time. They'd slept a few hours and then been awakened by bodies that were fully aroused and clamoring for more. They'd moved together, slowly, sleepily, matching each other's rhythm as if they'd been practicing for a lifetime— without thought for the consequences.

When she woke again, dawn was breaking. She snuggled into the arms that held her, breathing in the smell of sex and Rashid, sighing, loving, knowing there would never be anyone else for her but this man.

She stretched and slid away, dressing quickly in the dim light of early morning and hurried back to her room.

When she went down to breakfast an hour later, Karen, Abu-Khan, and Rashid were already in the small family dining room. Rashid was talking on his cell phone.

What was going on? Rashid put the phone in his pocket and turned to Olivia, his voice pained. "I have to go to Washington, DC. I have a meeting tomorrow to discuss a possible contract with the CIA. I can just make the next flight if I hurry."

He went to pack, leaving Olivia dazed and full of

questions. Half an hour later, she found herself standing beside one of Abu-Khan's limousines with Abu-Khan, Karen, and Nur, saying goodbye to Rashid. He kissed Abu-Khan's cheeks, hugged Nur, and briefly squeezed Karen's hand, leaving Olivia for last. When it was her turn to say goodbye, he grasped her by the shoulders but then seemed unable to speak. Everyone was waiting. Finally he kissed her on the cheek, a feather-brush of a kiss, and whispered into her ear. "Call me when you get to Juilliard. I'll visit you there."

And then he was gone.

She didn't hear from him in the first two weeks after he left, and she didn't try to call, but it was okay. She'd be back in the States in six weeks and would see him then.

When she suspected she was pregnant, she confided in Karen, who knew all about such things because she'd been trying to get pregnant ever since she married Abu-Khan. Karen produced a home pregnancy test that confirmed Olivia was indeed pregnant.

Then she did try to reach Rashid. She had Abu-Khan's secretary place a call to him as soon as she knew for sure, but the secretary told her there was no answer. She tried again the next day and the next day after that, and she would have kept trying, but Abu-Khan had started talking about the details of Rashid's wedding. It seemed final plans were being made.

Then the pressure to let Karen and Abu-Khan adopt the baby began.

****

Rashid drove with his left hand, not wanting to disturb Olivia by moving his right arm. The weight of her body and head against him felt like trust and promise. He absorbed it. He thought of the night to come—the *nights* to come—when they would be sleeping beside each other in a nomad tent. Other parts of his body yearned to also feel her weight.

Jamal woke in a foul mood, and his whining cry woke Olivia.

"He needs a diaper change," she said, "and he's hungry."

"Yes, I know. So am I, and I'm sure you are too. I'll watch for a place to stop as soon as we get off the highway."

At last he reached the dirt road that led to the nomad camp. A sense of triumph flooded through him. "We've made it, Livie. The dangerous part of the trip is behind us. All we have to do now is cross those mountains, and we'll be safe."

He stopped in a village to buy food for another picnic and to get gas. The station was as primitive as the first one. Olivia stood by the car watching the men pump the gas by hand. There were four of them, all wearing long, loose shirts, baggy cotton pants, and turbans. It was a laborious procedure that involved pulling on a long handle attached to a barrel of fuel.

About two miles after the village, they came to a place where a small river crossed the road. Rashid took off his shoes and socks, rolled up his pants, and waded across to see how deep it was. They could make it. After driving through the water, he stopped the car. "We can eat here by the river," he said. "You don't need to wear your chador. I don't think anyone will come along, but keep it nearby just in case."

While he set up a basin for washing, heated water for tea, and laid out a rug, Olivia and Jamal went down to wade in the water. The puppy waited at the water's edge, yipping his frustration at being left behind but unwilling to get wet. Livie looked like a wood sprite with her soft, pale hair stirring in the breeze and her long arms moving gracefully through the air. She caught him watching her and smiled her sprite's smile. Was she thinking about the night to come?

"How much farther do we have to go?" she asked when she and Jamal came to sit on the rug. The puppy attacked a bone Rashid had set out a few feet away.

"It's only about twenty more miles, but it will take at least an hour. Are you tired? Is your back hurting?"

"No, I'm fine. I was just curious."

He cut up portions of bread, cheese, and melon for each of them. "I still have your money, by the way. Do you want me to keep it until we get to Tehran?"

"Oh, the money." She seemed to have forgotten about it. "Yes, keep it. Thank you."

"I think it would be a good idea if you let me hold the ring too. It might make people curious."

She bit her lower lip. "You're right. It would draw attention. Yes, please keep it for me."

When she didn't move to take the ring off, he asked, "Well?"

"You mean right now?"

"Well, yes, right now would be as good a time as any. I'll take good care of it, Livie."

"I know you will. I wasn't worried about that." She pulled it off her finger and held it out to him, looking everywhere but at him.

What did this handing over the symbol of Abu-Khan's influence really mean to her?

Rashid took the ring and slipped it into his pocket.

"It's kind of surprising Abu-Khan didn't give it to Karen."

Olivia was sitting with her legs crossed. She took a bite of the juicy yellow melon. "She may have worn it; I wouldn't have noticed. He let her wear whatever she wanted of his family jewelry, and he gave her new things too. They both loved to shop."

"Was Karen happy? Did she really love Abu-Khan?"

Olivia thought for a moment before answering. "I know she loved the glamor of her life in the palace, and he obviously enjoyed having a beautiful, young American woman on his arm, but I'm not sure how much of an emotional connection they had. There may have been a bond I didn't see. Anyway, whatever they had must have been enough. They seemed happy."

"I hope they were. I always felt responsible for their meeting, you know. Karen used to come to our house with my sister during college breaks when they were freshmen. It was my idea for them to go to Behruz that summer, but I never imagined what would happen. It must have been quite a whirlwind courtship."

Olivia laughed. "It's funny to think of Abu-Khan reduced to the role of *suitor*, but Karen was quite a flirt when she was young; she would have known how to string him along."

Rashid cut off another hunk of bread for Jamal. "Well at least Abu-Khan finally got the heir his first two wives failed to give him."

"Yes, the much-needed heir." Her tone was bitter. "Was that why he divorced his first two wives? Was it because they couldn't give him children?"

"He didn't divorce his first wife. She died about

five years after they married. It was an arranged marriage, a politically advantageous one, and they were very young, but he seemed to love her. I don't think he would have divorced her."

"And his second wife?"

"That marriage was probably a mistake, the result of a momentary infatuation. She was an Iranian film star, and she seemed to find life in the palace rather boring. I think Abu-Khan would have stayed with her if she'd gotten pregnant, but since she didn't, I imagine they were both ready to end it."

Olivia took a sip of tea. "Karen was afraid he'd divorce her if she didn't have a baby. Do you suppose he would have?"

"I don't know. Most men would have started to think the problem lay with themselves, not with their wives. That's what I thought. I was surprised when I heard Karen was pregnant."

Olivia's eyes rounded with alarm, and she set the teacup down so quickly the contents sloshed onto the rug. Now what had he said? She was a minefield of subjects that triggered anxiety or anger. She was dabbing at the spilled tea with her napkin.

"Don't worry about it. It's just an old rug. It's probably been washed in the river a hundred times."

Jamal toddled toward the water, and the puppy abandoned his bone to follow. Rashid jumped to his feet to join them. When they got to the river, he scooped the boy into the air and swung him around, flinging him up and then catching him. Jamal looked startled and seemed almost about to cry.

"I'm sorry," Rashid said. "I didn't mean to frighten you." He made his horseplay more gentle, and soon the boy was giggling with delight.

Rashid set the boy down on his feet. Then he took a stone and threw it into the river, making a small splash a few feet in front of them. He handed Jamal a small stone. "You can throw one too," he said, but Jamal just looked back at him confused. Rashid threw another stone. "Now it's your turn."

Suddenly understanding dawned. Jamal plopped his stone into the water just in front of them and squealed happily.

"Do you want another stone? You can find one yourself." Rashid pointed to a nice round one and Jamal picked it up. He threw it and then another one and another, hooting and giggling and waiting for Rashid's approval after each splash. A particularly heavy stone dropped into the shallow water inches in front of his toes, splashing water onto his body and Rashid's legs. Jamal looked up warily as if he expected to be scolded.

"Nice one. Good job." Rashid gave the boy a smile of encouragement. Jamal laughed and bent to pick up another stone.

Olivia was wiping tears from her cheeks with the palms of her hands when Rashid returned to the rug with Jamal on his shoulders and the puppy circling his feet.

"What is it? Is your back hurting?"

"No." She picked up a napkin and mopped her face. "I'm just thinking about how much Jamal has missed."

"I hope I can make up for some of what he's missed, at least for a few days." He lowered Jamal to the ground and helped Olivia to her feet. "Maybe I can make up a little for what you've missed too."

What kind of life had it been for her? She was so easily moved by the tiniest of freedoms. "Can you relax for a while, Livie? Everything's going to work out. You'll see."

He pulled her to him and kissed her forehead. She lowered her eyelids, and he placed a solemn kiss on each of them. Then she turned her face up to his, asking, *begging*, for more. Okay. More. He kissed her. It was a deep, sober kiss that seemed to seal a bond between them. It was as if his every cell knew her and responded to her, as if it were her blood flowing through his veins. It was so elemental it stunned him. "You still feel it, don't you Livie."

She whispered *yes*.

He pulled her against his chest and pressed her head against his shoulder, stroking her hair and her face, murmuring that everything was going to be all right.

Was everything going to be all right?

It would be, he was sure, if she would only confide in him. She'd come with him. She'd given him the money and the ring. And she'd responded to his kisses with a fervor that had his blood still surging thick and hot through his veins. It was a start.

He just had to be patient.

****

Back in the car, Olivia ran her fingers over her now empty finger. Rashid had been right—the ring would have drawn attention—but it had been a huge leap of faith to take it off. She'd lived for so long with Abu-Khan's threats and had submitted so totally to them, that even now, even in this remote place, it felt that Abu-Khan might appear out of the sky to take Jamal if she defied him.

She could hear his booming voice demanding to know, *Where is the ring?*

But she'd done it. Taking off the ring and turning it over to Rashid had felt momentous. A sense of freedom had shivered through her, making her raw and new.

The road became rocky and bumpy, and it went up and down over an endless series of small rises like a roller coaster. Olivia had to hold herself braced against the floorboards and the door to keep from bouncing all over the interior of the car. Jamal was in a cranky mood, whining in boredom and trying to free himself from the straps that held him. Olivia got into the backseat and tried to amuse him with peekaboo games and toys, but no distraction lasted more than a few minutes, and after a while her own discomfort and a growing queasiness made it impossible to focus her attention on him. She gave up. He cried for a while and then lapsed into a sad, hiccupping whimper. The puppy, who lay between them, sighed his own little whines of sympathy.

Finally Rashid pointed out that their destination was in sight. A cluster of black tents dotted the rounded foothill ahead. A jeep was cutting across the slope toward them, dust billowing behind it. "That will be Saddiq coming to meet us. He's probably been watching the progress of our dust cloud for the last five miles."

When their vehicles met, the men got out to embrace and talk for a few minutes, and Rashid introduced Saddiq to Olivia. Saddiq was a short, muscular man of about forty, wearing the typical long shirt of the region and a wool vest. He greeted Olivia warmly and then, urged on by Rashid, hurried back to his vehicle to lead them to the camp.

The men and boys stood in a row, waiting to greet them, while the women and girls, all in colorful costumes, stood behind them. The camp consisted of about twenty tents in a large circle with a fire pit in the center. Camels, horses, and donkeys were tethered nearby, and sheep grazed on a grassy slope beyond.

When they came to a stop behind Saddiq's jeep, Rashid jumped out and hurried to release Jamal and the puppy. Jamal stopped whining as soon as his feet hit the ground; he toddled toward the row of nomads, stopping a few feet away to study them. They returned his gaze.

Olivia let her head fall back against the car seat and closed her eyes while Rashid talked to Saddiq. Smells of animal dung, wood smoke, and cooking meat wafted into the car. She stayed as she was, enjoying stillness after the rough ride, inhaling the earthy smells.

"I'm so sorry," Rashid said.

Olivia sat up at once, anxious for him to see she was all right, and swung her legs out of the car.

"I'm fine, really," she said, but before she could stand on her own, Rashid swept her into his arms and carried her past the astonished nomads to the smallest of the tents.

He laid her on a rug inside, but she immediately sat up to look around. The tent was tall. Rashid could stand in the center without bending his head. The floor was covered with red carpets in bold nomad patterns.

"This is our tent. Saddiq had it set up for us."

"*Our* tent?" Olivia asked.

"Well, yes. They think we're a family. Again, it was the easiest explanation. And I wouldn't have asked for more than one tent anyway. It's enough of an inconvenience for them to make this one available."

"Oh, of course." Her pulse quickened. *Her days of living as if they were a family weren't over.* Blood rushed to her face and to other, more intimate parts of her body. She and Rashid would be sharing a tent!

Rashid rubbed the back of his neck. He seemed to be studying the pattern of one of the rugs. "Don't worry, Livie. Since the nomad bedding is pretty rough, I've brought sleeping bags for all three of us. With your own sleeping bag to curl up in and with Jamal in here as chaperone, you should be safe from my animal urges."

Actually, it was her own urges she needed to fear, not his. Or, more precisely, it was what would happen if she gave in to those urges. Only the tiniest shred of discipline kept her from blurting out her whole story. She had to keep as much distance as possible between them—physical distance and emotional distance—or that tiny shred would be blasted to smithereens.

"Jamal could sleep between us," she suggested.

Rashid sighed and agreed." I don't want you to worry about anything, Livie. I want you to rest. Honestly, if I'd known the trip would be this hard on you, I wouldn't have attempted it...although I don't know what else I could have done."

"I'm all right, really. I'm just tired. I'll be fine tomorrow."

"Good. I'll bring your sleeping bag and some tea. Is there anything else you want? Are you hungry?"

"A little. What about Jamal? After sleeping so much in the car, he won't be tired for hours."

"Don't worry about him. I've asked Saddiq to be sure he's taken care of. He'll have half a dozen women watching his every move."

"Well, bring him to me if he needs me."

"Don't worry, I will. But I think what he needs right now is to be active. He'll be fine."

Two of the nomad women brought a basin of warm water for Olivia and then, after lowering the tent flap, squatted in the corner, giggling and whispering in the Qashami language while she splashed water onto her face and washed her hands. When the women had gone, Rashid returned with a steaming cup of tea and a plate of lamb meat and bread.

The meat smelled delicious, and it tasted as good as it smelled. She ate greedily while Rashid came and went, bringing things from the car.

He handed her a flashlight. "The toilet facilities are pretty basic. I hope you don't mind. Go to the other side of the car if you need to go out tonight. Tomorrow the women will show you where they go."

She sat on one of the rugs while Rashid arranged the sleeping bags, one long khaki-colored one on each side and a short one with Superman pictures printed on it in the middle. "Where did you get all these foreign things, the clothes you gave me, the car seat, and the sleeping bags?"

Rashid chuckled. "In the bazaar in Behruz City, believe it or not. You can buy just about anything there if you're willing to pay the price."

"I do appreciate it," Olivia said, aware again of how much she was in his debt.

"There's no need to say that, Olivia. I don't want your gratitude. I just want to see you safely out of this country. I was glad to pick up a few things for you. Did I get everything you need? Do you have something to wear in bed?"

She didn't have anything, since she'd left the gown Sarat loaned her in her room that morning. "No, but it doesn't matter. I can sleep in my clothes."

"There's no need to do that." He rummaged in his bag until he found a shirt of the style worn by the nomad men. He handed it to her. "Here, wear this. If you need anything else, I'll be outside by the fire." He picked up the teacup and plate and left, lowering the tent flap behind him.

It was dusk, and a few stars were already visible in the broad expanse of sky when Olivia slipped out to go to the bathroom. Afterward, she stood unnoticed by the tent for a while, watching the cheerful scene around the fire. They were all eating, and the puppy was going around the circle, begging for and being given tidbits of food. Jamal and Rashid were seated next to each other on a rug. Rashid was talking, telling some kind of story. Every now and then he paused while Saddiq translated his words into the nomad language and everyone laughed.

Her heart thumped happy anticipation. Tomorrow she would take her place with the others. Beside Rashid.

She slipped back into the tent and changed into Rashid's shirt. Then she slid into the flannel warmth of the sleeping bag and fell asleep.

Chapter Eight

Rashid awoke slowly the next morning, realizing, as if in a dream, that Livie was lying beside him. Livie. With her head on his shoulder and her arm slung across his chest. *His woman.* Her breath ruffled the hair on his chest. His heart swelled with a visceral reaction to her beauty. She'd had freckles on her nose when she was younger, but now they were gone, leaving her skin as clear and pure as a baby's. Her hair, long and straight and silky soft, was stretched across his bare chest. He wanted to weave his hands into it. He wanted to throw his leg over her. His body surged to life, ready to claim her, but he didn't move.

She sighed and stretched, arching her back, and then pressed her body more tightly against him. She shifted her arm from his chest to his hair. Her legs moved restlessly. Seeking his? Damn the two layers of sleeping bags that separated them. He wanted her wrapped around him, her legs clasping his.

Finally, her eyes fluttered open. He smiled. She smiled. He kissed the top of her head, her forehead, her nose. Her mouth, which didn't open but still melted against his.

He broke the kiss and reached for the zipper of his sleeping bag. "I need to brush my teeth," she whispered, and they both laughed. She was reaching too, groping with her own zipper, but then suddenly she stopped.

She raised herself up on her elbows and looked around the tent. "Where's Jamal?"

"He's fine. Don't worry. He slept in Saddiq's tent last night. He played with Saddiq's five-year-old son after dinner, and after a while they both fell asleep. I didn't see any need to move him."

"Oh." She looked down at the bright blue and red print of the Superman sleeping bag, which was lying still flat and unoccupied beneath her. She blushed. She must be imagining, as Rashid was, how she'd managed to roll and squirm across it while still in her sleeping bag and still asleep. To be with him.

"Come back to me." He reached for her shoulder.

"No, I can't. I shouldn't have…" She slithered out of the bag without bothering to undo the zipper and stood up.

She took off her briefs and pulled on a clean pair, followed by jeans, all under cover of the long nomad shirt. When she'd secured the jeans, she turned her back and unbuttoned the shirt. She glanced over her shoulder and saw him watching. "You could turn away, you know."

"Oh no." He shook his head. "That would not be possible."

She scowled, no doubt trying to look indignant but only managing to be provocative. And adorable. She drew her arms from the sleeves, leaving the shirt hanging from her shoulders while she pulled a sweater over her head. She allowed the shirt to fall to the floor, and then she turned back to face him, fully dressed. It had all been accomplished with her usual dancer's grace and the sleight of hand of a magician.

He brought his hands together three times, silently clapping. "That was far more tantalizing than a regular striptease."

She was irresistible. She was magnificent. Her nipples were visible beneath the soft fabric of the sweater, hard, straining toward him. She hesitated when she saw his gaze glide over them. Her cheeks blazed. "You should have gotten me a bra."

"You don't need one, Livie." He couldn't take his eyes away from the swell of her breasts; he couldn't resist teasing her. "You'd be the only woman in the camp wearing one. I'm sure you'd feel quite conspicuous."

She glared at him. "You didn't used to enjoy making me uncomfortable."

That was true. What was wrong with him? He was an oaf. He was acting like a teenager. "I'm sorry, Livie. I don't want to make you uncomfortable. It's just that I'm so damned frustrated, trying to figure out why you're afraid to trust me and why you're determined to deny your feelings. If I needle you, it's because I'm willing to do anything to get an honest reaction from you."

His gaze drifted down to her breasts again, but this time, instead of embarrassing *her* with his appraisal, he felt embarrassed himself.

"I'm sorry too," she said.

She said it simply and sincerely. She was sorry. Whatever it was that made her hold back from him was not arbitrary and not trivial. It was a serious problem, at least to her. He had to contain his frustration, and his libido too, and watch for ways to regain her trust.

She was looking around the tent. "I must have left

my chador in the car. Could you get it for me?"

"You won't need a chador while we're crossing the mountains," Rashid told her. "You'll be wearing the same kind of clothes as the nomad women, with a scarf over your hair in case any soldiers see us from a distance. You can pull the scarf across your face if any outsiders come near."

"Oh. Where am I going to get this costume?"

"Saddiq's wife and the other women bought the materials and made the clothes. They'll give them to you when you go to Saddiq's tent. I believe they're quite anxious to see how you like them."

Anticipation glowed on her face. "Oh. I should hurry then."

"No, you don't have to hurry. We're staying here today so you can rest up and get used to the altitude before we continue with the trip."

She sat down on the rug and began putting on her sandals. "How do you happen to know Saddiq?"

"We were at UCLA together. He's Qashami, but his father left the tribe to become a merchant and Saddiq was raised in Behruz City. He used to spend his summers with his grandfather, so he knows the nomad way of life. He teaches at Behruz University now, but since Abu-Khan closed the university five weeks ago, he and his family are spending a few months with his relatives."

She'd finished putting on her sandals. Now she sat cross-legged, brushing her hair. "Is his wife Qashami too?"

"Yes. They've known each other since they were children."

The fabric of her sweater slid over her breasts as

she reached with her long, graceful arms to yank at a tangle. Her movements were like an erotic dance. Rashid was captivated. And turned on. He wanted to take her right then.

Patience.

She paused with her arms raised to her hair. "What do these people think?" she asked. "What have you told them about me?"

"I told Saddiq the truth. I hope you don't mind. I trust him absolutely. He told the others a story about how some powerful government official is trying to steal you from me so he can have you as his bride. This seems plausible to them. They don't have a very good opinion of government officials. They're happy to help us escape the evil would-be wife stealer. If anyone asks them if they've seen a foreign woman crossing the mountains, they'll swear they haven't."

She gasped and was silent for a moment. Then she laughed quietly and returned to her work with the hairbrush. The tangle yielded and her hair settled into its usual sleek mane down her back.

She raised herself up, spinning and unfolding herself in her dancer's way. "Okay then. It's time for me to start my life as a guest-member of the Qashami tribe."

She looked ready for adventure. She looked happy. She looked like his old Livie.

****

Cool mountain air and a dazzling clear blue sky greeted Olivia when she left the warmth of the tent. She asked two men who were sitting by the still-smoldering embers of the fire which tent was Saddiq's, and they pointed to the far side of the encampment.

Walking in public without a chador made her feel liberated and carefree. She smiled at everyone, and they nodded or smiled shyly back. She was eager to join the women, eager to be part of something.

As she walked toward Saddiq's tent, she considered the role she was playing. The nomads thought they were a family. They thought a government official was trying to steal her from Rashid. It was so much closer to the truth than Rashid could ever guess. The idea of living an act that was nearly the truth thrilled her.

The puppy yapped when he saw her, but he didn't leave his post by the opening of Saddiq's tent, where he was apparently "on duty" guarding Jamal. He wagged his tail furiously when she bent to pet him, and he tried to follow her into the tent, but he was quickly evicted by one of the men. Jamal was there, already dressed, sitting with three other children, eating breakfast. When he saw Olivia, he reached to be lifted into her arms. Saddiq's wife Fatima introduced herself and the other women and then motioned for Olivia to sit on the rug next to her.

She sat with Jamal in her lap and was served a breakfast of flat bread, yogurt and tea. Fatima, who was the only one who spoke Farsi, translated when the others wanted to know her and Jamal's ages. There was a great deal of murmured discussion when Olivia said she was twenty-three.

Fatima refilled Olivia's teacup. "They thought you were about fourteen. And they think you're too thin. They're going to make a special pudding to help fatten you up."

"That's very kind." Olivia gave them all a friendly

smile.

When the meal was over, the women helped her put on her new costume. They wanted to do everything. Their hands were all over her, pulling at her sweater and trying to open the snap and zipper of her jeans. They giggled and exclaimed when they saw her small, pale breasts, but the biggest source of delight turned out to be her lacy briefs. She was relieved when they covered her with the new clothes.

The bright colors and the enthusiasm of the women as they dressed and preened her made her feel like a child getting ready for a special party. First they helped her put on two gauzy petticoats, then a skirt and, finally, a blouse. The skirt was a gathered and tiered patchwork of pink, red, yellow, and purple cotton that fell almost to the ground. The blouse—which was white with red and purple embroidery—was gathered around a scooped neck and had full sleeves that came to tight bands at her wrists. The final touches consisted of an embroidered purple sash, which they tied around her waist, and a lace-trimmed mantle of white silk that covered her hair. The mantle was held in place by a purple headband tied across her forehead.

Olivia enjoyed a borrowed sense of belonging, something she hadn't felt for a long time. She was surrounded by women wearing costumes similar to hers who were all beaming with pride at her appearance. The only difference between her costume and theirs was that the other women wore jangly silver jewelry.

She'd admired the nomad women she'd seen in the city. They stood so tall and moved with such confidence. Now, dressed like them, she stood taller herself. Her own sense of pride and confidence swelled.

The women were waiting for her reaction. She took a few steps away, feeling the swish of the petticoats around her legs, and then she stretched out her arms and did a pirouette that lifted the skirt into a rippling circle of color around her. She smiled at the women, grateful for the sense of sisterhood they shared with her. She was aware of her body in a new way. The costume made her feel womanly as nothing she had worn before ever had, but at the same time it made her feel frivolous.

"Tell them it's beautiful. Thank them for me," she said, and Fatima translated her praise. "Everything fits perfectly. How did you know my size?"

"Your husband told me. I met him in Behruz City last week. He gave me the sizes when he gave me money to buy the materials."

"Did you buy this too?" She fingered the delicate lace of the mantle. It was exquisite compared to the plain cotton ones worn by the other women.

"Your husband asked me to get you a mantle such as this."

Olivia flushed with pleasure at the idea of Rashid taking a personal interest in her costume. How would he react when he saw her in it?

"This reminds me of a wedding," Fatima said when they all stepped out of the tent. "When a Qashami girl gets married, the women all help her dress in her wedding clothes and then they escort her to her husband's tent."

Walking toward the tent of her "husband," Olivia felt like a bride. The mantle framed her face and fell down her back like a bride's veil, and the long skirt swayed with every step. Rashid stood in front of the

126

tent talking to Saddiq. He was wearing a long shirt and a wool vest like those worn by the other men. He was holding up a rifle, sighting along the barrel. He said something to Saddiq and handed him the rifle; then he turned and saw the procession of women approaching. Time stopped for several heartbeats when his eyes fell on Olivia. He seemed to straighten up, to become taller, and everything about him became very still.

She met his gaze boldly. The petticoats swished around her legs when she walked. She felt the swing of her arms, the sway of her hips, even the slight bounce of her breasts.

By the time she reached Rashid and Saddiq, she had a serious case of nerves that fit quite well with the bridal image Fatima had evoked. All the women stood behind her, waiting for Rashid's reaction.

"Spin around again like you did for us in the tent," Fatima whispered to Olivia.

Rashid's nomad clothes made him look primitive and very male. His eyes were intent on her, like the eyes of an animal watching its prey. He was motionless except for a slight quivering of his nostrils.

Olivia lifted her arms slowly, and the women stepped back away from her. Then she began the pirouette. She moved as if in a trance. Everything seemed to happen in slow motion. But still the skirt rose, its colors blurring as she spun, and she felt dizzy and flushed when she stopped. She gave Rashid a smile that came from some new knowledge.

"You are a temptress," he said in English. His eyes were dark pools that beckoned her to tempt and be tempted.

"The ladies are waiting to see what you think of

their handiwork."

He stepped toward her and reached his hand up to touch her face at her temple. Then he slid it down until it cupped the nape of her neck. A shiver of response rippled through her, but she didn't move.

"She is very beautiful," he said in Farsi. "The costume is perfect. She is perfect." He kissed her lightly on the lips. The speculations and remarks of the nomads hushed. A crow cawed in the distance, and then it was silent too. She was mesmerized. She felt possessed.

"I have something for you," he said.

Olivia and the nomad women watched curiously as he reached into the pocket of his vest, pulled out a cloth bag, and emptied it into his hand.

He offered the gift to her on his open palm. It was a pair of silver bracelets made of large links, each of which held a bell. The bells were covered with a delicate pattern of lines and dots, etched and soldered to form flowers. They were old: the details of the flowers were worn smooth and shiny with age, and the indented areas were dark with layers of tarnish.

"They're beautiful," Olivia was stunned by the bold beauty of the bracelets. "Where did you get them?"

"From one of the antique dealers in Behruz City."

She handed them back to him and held out her arms so he could put them on her wrists, but he knelt down in front of her. "They're ankle bracelets."

The Qashami women murmured their approval while he placed a bracelet on one ankle and then the other, carefully closing the clasp on each. The metal was cold, but his hands were warm. His breath fanned her legs as he bent over his task.

"Thank you," she said when he stood facing her again. "You shouldn't have bought them. It wasn't necessary."

His eyes gleamed satisfaction. "I know it wasn't necessary, but I wanted you to have them. I liked them. I wanted you to feel authentic in your costume."

A twinge of self-consciousness rippled through her. She was too affected by the costume. The bright colors were too bold and uninhibited; the whole thing was too much a statement of raw femininity. It seemed her old clothes had hidden her female needs and instincts while these clothes accentuated them, making every movement an erotic act.

"Come for a walk with me." He put his arm across her shoulder and drew her to his side. He said to Saddiq. "I'm going to take Olivia to see the waterfall you told me about. We'll be back before lunch."

"What about Jamal?" Olivia asked. He was squatting on the ground in front of Saddiq's tent, surrounded by nomad children of all ages. Each child held a small plastic car, no doubt a gift from Rashid. They were pushing the cars through the dust, making engine sounds and laughing.

"Don't worry," Saddiq said. "We'll take care of him."

Rashid led her away from the camp, his arm draped over her shoulders. When they came to a small hill, he lowered his arm and took her hand. The bells of her ankle bracelets tinkled softly with each step.

"Don't let me go too fast," he said. "I don't want you to get tired."

She sucked the cool, mountain air deep into her lungs. Pressure that had been holding her down somehow lifted; she felt she could fly. The vastness and openness of the landscape made her feel breathless. Their eyes met and held and they both stopped walking as if in response to some silent signal. A gust of wind wafted the mantle about her face and pressed the skirt against her legs.

She waited for him to kiss her, lips quivering, but he didn't move. He studied her, seeing the turbulence inside her. There was a calm about him, a quiet sense of waiting that communicated itself to her through the warm, firm grasp of his hand. She smiled a tremulous smile. It seemed a great act of courage to keep returning his gaze, to stand so near to him with their hands clasped, to smile at him openly. She felt courageous.

"Well then," he said after a while, speaking as if some important issue had been resolved, "let's continue with our walk."

They came to a small stream and turned west to walk along its rocky bank. The land sloped gently up toward a cliff that marked the beginning of the foothills. A beautiful oasis of green spread on either side of the stream at the base of the cliff. Sheep, horses, donkeys, and camels grazed there, all under the watchful eyes of two young nomad men.

They entered a grove of poplar trees at the base of the cliff. The herdsmen and the animals were no longer in sight, but the sounds of bleating sheep and the clanging of bells could still be heard. The leaves of the poplar trees rustled overhead and cascading water burbled somewhere beyond the grove.

They reached the place where the stream came down a high cliff and formed a pool of clear water at the base.

"Would you like to bathe?" Rashid asked.

With dust from the previous day's trip still on her skin and in her hair, the idea sounded almost irresistible, but weren't the herdsmen too close? And what would Rashid be doing while she was in the water?

"I have shampoo and soap," Rashid said, tantalizing her even more. "I'll go to the edge of the trees to make sure no one comes near. Unless you want me to stay. I wouldn't mind seeing another peekaboo performance like the one I saw this morning."

She blushed but ignored his taunt. "It sounds heavenly. And I'd appreciate it if you'd watch for the shepherds."

He took a small plastic bottle of shampoo and a cake of soap from his pocket and pressed them into her hand; then he bent and brushed his lips across hers. The passion that had been simmering ever since she woke that morning flared sharp in her womb. He felt it too; desire darkened his eyes. But he walked away and disappeared between the trees.

Olivia stripped down to her briefs, laying her clothes carefully on a flat rock. She left the ankle bracelets on. The water was cold, but she waded into it quickly. She slid the soap up and down her arms and legs and all over her body, luxuriating in the pleasure of feeling clean, and then she lathered her hair. She was lying on her back with the shampoo bottle and soap tucked into her briefs when she heard a splash near the waterfall. She dropped her feet to the bottom and stood, folding her arms across her breasts, and looked around, but she saw nothing. Then suddenly strong hands gripped her ankles. It was Rashid. A distorted, wavy image of his naked body stretched out before her at her feet.

"No," she whispered, although the most intimate parts of her body were clamoring *yes*. His hands caressed the outside of her legs, her thighs, her hips and then her rib cage until they came to grasp her under the arms. Nerves came to tingling life wherever he touched. Prickles of fire coursed along tiny capillaries to her womb and her breasts and her heart.

"You promised to watch out for the shepherds," she said when at last he stood facing her.

He gave her a smile of mock apology. "I did that *while you were undressing*, but now you're hidden by the water. And I need a bath too. You don't think it's fair that you should be the only one to enjoy the water, do you?" He shifted his hands up until his thumbs reached the outer swell of her breasts. Desire jolted through her, making her legs suddenly weak, and she lifted her arms to grasp his shoulders.

"Rashid," she moaned. "Please..."

"Livie. Oh God, Livie." His arms came around her and he pulled her against him. His hands moved through the water over the slickness of her wet skin, stroking, sliding over her shoulders, down along her back to her waist and to the strip of fabric that crossed her bottom. Every inch of skin he touched blazed to life. She pressed her breasts against the muscles of his chest and her thighs against his thighs and her belly against his hard need. Nothing was enough. She turned her face blindly up to him and his lips came down to hers in a searing kiss.

Then suddenly he pulled away. "Did you hear something?" he asked.

"No. What?" *No, don't stop.*

"Livie, I'm sorry." His eyes were still glazed with desire. "I didn't mean for this to happen, not here, not now. I should have let you bathe by yourself. I should have known… God, don't look at me like that. I want you so badly I'm going crazy, but this is not the place. The herdsmen are near. I hear the bells of the animals."

She clung to him. What? Herdsmen? She was so stunned by the force of feelings that had literally almost knocked her off her feet that she couldn't react to his sudden change of subject

"Wait until tonight." He gave her one more light kiss.

Tonight. Was she ready? Did she dare? Would she be able to hold back her secrets if she made love with him?

He asked for the soap and shampoo.

She splashed water on her flushed cheeks and then reached into her briefs. After handing him the soap and shampoo, she swam to deeper water, where she drifted and swam while Rashid soaped his body and lathered his hair.

"You stay here," he said when he was done. "I'll stand at the edge of the trees to make sure no one comes while you're dressing."

He walked toward the bank, displaying no self-consciousness at all as inch by inch his naked body was revealed. He still played soccer; he still had the build of an athlete. She looked at the lean, muscled shape of his buttocks when he reached up to take his clothes from the branch of a tree where he'd left them. She turned away after only a few seconds, but the image of him in that pose was etched permanently on her brain. It came to her unbidden while she swam in the pool and then, when he was gone from sight, while she dressed.

Wait until tonight.

Chapter Nine

Rashid saw Olivia sitting on a rock at the edge of the pool when he came back through the grove of poplars. She was dressed again except for the mantle and her sandals, and she was leaning back against her arms, her face turned up to the sun. His breath caught as it had in the palace courtyard two years before.

"Are the herdsmen still there?" she asked when he reached her.

"Yes, they're moving this way, but they're not close enough to have seen anything."

Color rose to her cheeks. Was she thinking about what they might have seen? He remembered the feel of her eager body pressed against his, and his own body pulsed to life once again. *Just a few more hours.* Soon they would be alone in the tent. Well, alone except for Jamal, but he was a sound sleeper. Surely tonight she would surrender to the feelings she'd been so intent on denying. They would have to be quiet, but he could do that. Making love with Olivia would be a form of worship, solemn and sacred.

He sat down on the rock beside her. "You blush very prettily, you know. It's a bit more subtle now than it was when you were younger. I remember once you came to the dinner table wearing lipstick and Abu-Khan scolded you. He asked for my opinion, so I looked at you, trying to evaluate the effect, and while I was looking, the most amazing transformation occurred. Before I answered his question, your face had become almost the same color as the lipstick."

"I was seventeen. I'm surprised you remember. Karen laughed when Abu-Khan scolded me. I was furious with both of them for treating me like a child in front of you."

"Oh, I remember very well. You were wearing a turquoise dress with ruffles around the neck, which was unusual for you; you were such a tomboy. The lipstick was subtle, and you looked pretty. I thought Abu-Khan was unkind and Karen was insensitive, but I didn't say anything for fear of making things worse."

Her cheeks seemed to be blazing. "Oh you thought I was pretty? I wish you'd told me. It would have helped me get past my embarrassment. I was thinking of you when I put that lipstick on."

"Oh really? I never guessed."

"Oh come on, I'm sure you knew I had a crush on you."

"No, I didn't." She'd had a crush on him? Really? He'd never thought of her in that way, not until two years ago. "I thought you were a little princess who was above that kind of thing."

She laughed. "You must have been aware of how I felt."

He hadn't been. Knowing it now brought a ripple of satisfaction.

"I'm sorry Abu-Khan and Karen were so insensitive. I often wished Karen could have been more of a mother to you."

"She didn't know how to be a mother to an adolescent girl, but she would have been a good mother to Jamal. She and I were close in the end. Jamal brought us closer."

"How was it for you when she died?"

A shadow crossed Olivia's face. "It was hard, but I was busy with Jamal. I didn't have time to dwell on it."

"Tell me about your travels together. Where did you go? What did you do?"

Her eyes skittered to the waterfall and to the trees beyond and to the sky. "Travels?"

"I came back to see you a few months after that last time, and Abu-Khan told me you and Karen were traveling." Abu-Khan had made him feel like a fool for coming. He'd made it sound like Olivia's life was full of sophisticated fun. "Didn't he tell you I came?" Abu-Khan had also told him most emphatically that Olivia didn't want to see him.

She didn't answer. She had that ready-to-bolt look she'd had when he found her with the puppy. "He didn't tell you, did he." It was a statement, a realization, not a question. "I should have known, but at the time I trusted him. You know, he was a father figure for me after my own father died, very much as Karen was a mother figure for you."

"Yes, I know."

"Where were you then? Did he tell me the truth when he said you and Karen were traveling?"

"We were at the Summer Palace. I was…I mean, it was during the pregnancy."

"Ah, yes. I realized later that Karen was already pregnant then. So you were at the Summer Palace. The impression Abu-Khan gave was of a sort of jet-setting splurge in France." He'd been surprised that Abu-Khan would allow the women in his life such freedom, but he'd trusted him. "The Summer Palace makes more sense. Was Karen sick then? Did she know about her illness?"

"No. She was diagnosed when Jamal was a few weeks old. It was lung cancer. Six weeks later she was gone."

"Why did you stay in Behruz after I left if it wasn't because of Karen's illness? You were so excited about starting at Juilliard. What happened?"

She looked at the surface of the pool where it rippled away from the waterfall. She'd been strapping on her sandals, but now she was still. Neither of them moved. Camel bells and falling water combined together to make background music. The question and its implications ricocheted between them. "I don't know. I guess some sixth sense told me Karen needed me. And then, when I knew there was going to be a baby, I felt I should stay."

"I see," he said, but he didn't really. *Some sixth sense* didn't seem like a strong enough motive for her to give up her dream of going to Juilliard.

She finished with her sandals and rose to her feet. She began to arrange the mantle over her head.

"Wait." Rashid got up too and stood facing her. "Let me help." He pulled the mantle forward, adjusting it on the sides, tucking back wisps of hair that tried to escape. Her hair, like everything else, had dried quickly in the thin, dry air of the high plateau.

Rashid stroked her cheek with the tips of his fingers and then rested his hand against the side of her face. Her eyes were soft and vulnerable and yearning. She wanted him. Her reaction when he touched her was honest. She couldn't hide her desire. *Just a few more hours.* When he held her in his arms tonight, when they were both naked, when they slid together, her response then would be real. He could trust that. He could build on it.

Would she be able to keep holding in her secrets after that?

Maybe not.

Rashid lowered his hand from her face and took the purple band from her hand. He tied it around her head with shaking fingers. "You're very beautiful in your costume. You look like someone from another world, like a cross between a fairy and a gypsy."

He took her hand and led her back away from the waterfall toward the camp. They waved when they passed the herdsmen, but they didn't stop. They walked slowly, talking about the nomads.

"It was so kind of the women to make the costume for me," Olivia said. "Should I pay them?"

"No. They would be insulted if you offered. I had Fatima buy about three times as much material as was needed so the women could keep what was left over. I'm afraid that's all we can do, but don't worry. They enjoyed making it. They love having you with them in the camp."

They loved *her*, her sweetness and her beauty.

And so did he.

****

They found Jamal in Saddiq's tent. Fatima was serving lunch.

"I feel terrible about being waited on like this," Olivia whispered to Rashid. "Do you think she'd let me help?"

"No. Relax and enjoy being treated like royalty.

Your life as a commoner will begin when we get to the U.S."

Did he have a picture in his mind of her life in the U.S.? Had he made plans? Probably, but she wouldn't be able to go along with them. She didn't ask. She wasn't ready for *that* discussion.

For lunch they had wild pheasant the men had shot that morning. When they finished eating, women from one of the other tents brought rice pudding they'd prepared for Olivia. The women stood in the background watching as she began eating the large portion they'd brought her. She showed her appreciation with sign language, rubbing her stomach and smiling and nodding, even though the pudding was rich and she was already full.

Rashid was also given a serving, and he made a great show of appreciation, but he must have been full, judging by the look of appeal he gave Olivia when his back was turned to the women. "They really made this for you, so you should probably eat my portion as well." He held out his bowl to her.

"No, thank you." She gave him a saccharine smile.

After lunch Rashid helped Saddiq with repair work on the jeep, and Olivia sat by the embers of the previous night's fire trying to read. Jamal and the puppy wandered around the camp, finding the attention they both seemed to crave.

She had a hard time concentrating on her book. That morning's conversation with Rashid swirled in her mind.

He'd come back after he left two years ago, and Abu-Khan hadn't told her.

Had Karen known? No, she couldn't have. Karen

wouldn't have kept that information from Olivia. It had to be all Abu-Khan. His plot, his manipulation. Karen could have deluded herself into believing she was doing Olivia a favor by taking Jamal—Abu-Khan would have helped her justify that delusion—but she wouldn't have helped Abu-Khan convince Olivia that Rashid didn't care. Not unless she truly believed it. Karen had been a little self-absorbed, but she wasn't cruel. She'd loved Olivia.

Olivia cringed when she remembered her flimsy explanation about "some sixth sense" telling her to stay in Behruz. Rashid hadn't sounded convinced. She'd seen his analytical mind trying to fill in the blanks.

He was sucking her into his web, softening her with his concern, always gaining more and more pieces to the puzzle of her secret. He was seducing her with his flattery and with his touch until she was in a constant state of tingling awareness. Her defenses were crumbling, and he knew it.

Every nerve in her body was on stand-by alert. *Waiting for tonight.*

She napped with Jamal, the puppy wedged between them, and then she and Rashid took Jamal down to the stream for a bath. Rashid actually did all the work, and he was the one to get wet while Olivia sat on the bank watching and laughing and marveling about the rapport between the man and the boy.

Jamal rode on Rashid's shoulders on the way back to the camp. Olivia walked at Rashid's side, her hand firmly nested in his. They were bound together and separated from the rest of the world. It was the same later when she sat across the dinner cloth from him in Saddiq's tent. He talked to the others and laughed with them, and she helped Jamal with his food, but always there was a thrum of awareness between them. Every time his gaze came to rest on her, she saw the desire that smoldered beneath the surface and an answering pulse surged through her body.

Wait until tonight. She tried not to think about the small tent that awaited them, but by the time they were saying goodnight to the others she was trembling with anticipation.

Jamal would be there, *but Jamal would soon be asleep,* and then it would be just the two of them.

Jamal played with Saddiq's children after dinner. When Olivia went to pick him up, he squirmed in resistance and said the word, *Fawd.* She didn't know what he meant.

"He's trying to say *Faroud,*" Fatima explained. "That's the name of my five-year-old son. Jamal slept next to him last night, and it appears he wants to sleep here again tonight. You don't mind, do you?"

Oh! Had Rashid orchestrated this? No, he couldn't have. His expression was innocent. A little smug, but innocent. Olivia asked Jamal, "Is that what you want? You want to sleep here?"

"Fawd," he repeated, grinning his delight at having been understood.

"That's a good idea," Rashid said to Fatima. His eyes burned into Olivia, demanding everything, offering no escape. "Come along, Livie. Fatima has diapers and all the other things she needs. I gave her everything last night. Jamal will be fine."

She kissed her son goodnight and followed Rashid into the starlit night.

The puppy, who'd been outside the opening of the

tent gnawing on a lamb bone that was longer than he was, started to follow but stopped after a few feet and yipped a protest. When they kept walking, he yipped once more and then returned to work on his bone. He would stay with Jamal.

She brushed her teeth in a daze. The thinking part of her brain—the part that should have reminded her about the danger of becoming more intimate with Rashid—refused to function. When she entered the tent, Rashid was straightening their sleeping bags, zipping them together.

She waited just inside the opening while he finished the task. An oil lamp hanging from the roof pole of the tent cast a flickering light over everything. She had thought while she was outside walking and while she was brushing her teeth that she might still say *no*, but the desire on Rashid's tense face when he stood made a mockery of her hesitation. The oil lamp was reflected in his eyes, accentuating the resolve she saw there.

He must have seen when desire overcame doubt; she didn't try to hide it. She wanted him; she'd always wanted him. There would be no pretense.

Nomads were still moving about the camp, speaking Qashami, and sheep bleated in the distance. A camel let out a cry that sounded like a complaint. It all sounded far away. The world had constricted down to this tent, this man, this moment.

His movements were agonizingly slow but charged with determination as he opened the buttons of his shirt, sloughed it off, and dropped it to the floor. His arms suddenly fascinated her, especially the bulge of his biceps, the veins that stood out there, and the tan line that circled his upper arm. Seeing the muscles of his chest made her want to crush her breasts against him as she had in the pool. To rub against him and taste him.

He pulled down the nomad pants but left on his briefs, and she began the ritual of removing her own clothes.

First, after kicking off her sandals, she removed the headband and the mantle, folding them carefully and laying them on the rug at her feet. She untied the sash and began to pull up the blouse, but she stopped before her breasts were exposed, feeling both brazen and shy. Rashid was absolutely still, and for a moment she was too. Then a slight movement of his arm, a tensing of the muscle, brought her back to life, and she pulled the blouse over her head.

Rashid expelled his breath in a harsh, rasping gasp and then sucked his lungs full again. His rough breathing was the only sound in the tent. Olivia folded the blouse and dropped it at her feet. It took a while to remove the skirt and the petticoats—there were three buttons to be found and she was groping for them with fingers that had become very clumsy—but finally she undid the last one and the skirt and petticoats fell into a mound around her feet. She stood before him wearing nothing but her briefs and ankle bracelets.

"Come here," he said.

A shiver ran through her. The bells tinkled when she stepped toward him. The night air was cool on her flushed skin. The yearning on Rashid's face and the taut, waiting tension of his body seared through her. He lifted his hands and cupped her face.

"Livie." He moaned her name, and she knew their parting two years ago had been as painful for him as it had been for her.

"Rashid." Her voice was a whisper of love. She touched his face, saying with her fingers the words her lips could not speak. *I love you.* She stroked his cheek with her flattened palm, feeling the rough stubble of his beard and the tight clench of his jaw. "I'm so sorry." She moved her hand over his face, brushing her fingers across his lips. For two lonely years, she'd thought only of her own pain, but now she knew he had suffered too.

He grasped her hand and touched his lips to each of her knuckles, his eyes daring and promising at the same time. Then he lifted her into his arms and they kissed as they had on the bench in Reza's garden two years before, hot and eager and impatient. He tried to sit down on his sleeping bag, but it was awkward with her in his arms, and he collapsed at the end, throwing one hand onto the floor for balance and dropping Olivia into his lap. They laughed. They held each other and laughed. They looked into each other's eyes and laughed. Then laughter died and passion blazed.

Her hands circled his waist, gliding over the smooth hardness of his muscles. She straddled him, pressing against him in the most intimate way, and his body stirred beneath her. He moved his hands over her skin with growing urgency, threading his fingers into her hair, pulling her head back, kissing her hungrily. She moved against him, rocking, rubbing, seeking…more.

"Rashid, I don't have protection."

"Don't worry," he whispered.

She removed her one remaining garment while he did the same. He took the necessary precautions, and then moved with her down into the sleeping bag.

His hands swept up and down from her shoulders to her buttocks, molding her into his body. When his leg slid between her legs, a tremor shook through her and a sound like a plea escaped her lips.

He rolled her onto her back.

Now. She couldn't stand to wait another minute. Now, now, now. She arched up against him, reaching for hardness and pressure where she was most yearning.

"Livie, I'm sorry, I can't wait any longer. I've waited so long."

Don't wait. "Kiss me."

He kissed her, and she pulled herself up to him. Ahhh, the feel of his skin. His hardness against her softness. His heat enflaming her heat. She had her arms around him, and then her legs. The kiss went on and on. He entered her and kept kissing her, and in moments they both found blissful release.

She drifted back to earth while aftershocks of sensation pulsed through her. He settled beside her but still held her in his arms.

"I'm sorry I couldn't wait," he said.

"I didn't want you to wait," she said.

They laughed softly, their chests bumped together from the laughter, and that made them laugh even more.

Although the grip of his arms around her never slackened, his breathing fell into the peaceful rhythm of sleep. *I love you.* Her heart thumped to the rhythm of those words. *I love you I love you I love you.* She longed to say it aloud. She wanted to shout the words from the top of Gemdar Kuh. And she longed to tell Rashid about Jamal. How was she going to hold the truth in now? She'd known all along that if she gave herself to him then all her defenses would fall.

She must have dozed. When she woke up, the oil lamp had died, leaving the tent in darkness. Rashid was moving his hands slowly over her back, whispering sweet endearments, "darling" and "beloved" in Farsi. He brought his lips down to hers, claiming her in a series of tender kisses that grew deeper and more demanding. She quivered in response.

They made love again, trying to go more slowly, but the tension quickly built until they were both on fire, urgently seeking each other, seeking release. Sighing, laughing, embracing, finding release, and sleeping again.

Chapter Ten

Rashid woke to the sounds of activity in the camp: men yelling instructions to each other, camels groaning, and children shouting with excitement. He should be helping. But Livie was lying in his arms. His heart swelled with love and hope, and a profound feeling of protectiveness. *Livie was in his arms.* She had given herself to him so wholly, so sweetly, so passionately. Surely now...

Now what? His arms tightened around her. *Wake up. Tell me now what?* Would she tell him her secrets? Would she let him help her? *Could they plan a future together?* Because that was what he wanted. He wanted to awaken with her in his arms every day of his life.

He'd wondered all along if there was some trace of racism, or elitism, or *American*-ism that kept her from committing to him, but now he knew it couldn't have been that. Her surrender had been total. She'd let him see into her soul, and there was no judgment in her. There was something else holding her back. Surely now she would tell him. If it was her desire to be with Jamal, they would figure it out together. They could live in Behruz once peace had been restored. They could live in the palace or nearby. He would have to travel to California and Washington D.C. occasionally, but most of his work could be done by computer. His mind raced, busily solving the practicalities that would be involved, but he stopped himself. He would deal with all that when the time came. *If that was the problem. If it was the only problem.* Instinct told him it wasn't. She had to tell him.

She arched her back, stretching and straining toward him. He lifted her hair away from her face and whispered "good morning" into her ear.

She woke up and nestled down farther into the sleeping bag, burying her head in its warmth.

He laughed. "Come out of there. You're not hiding from me, not any more, not after last night." He pulled back the bag and nuzzled her neck. She wiggled away, but she couldn't go far, and soon he was on top of her, his legs astride her, his hands holding her arms pinned to her sides.

She turned her head from side to side, avoiding eye contact, but she was laughing too. She looked sleepy and shy and beautiful. She looked loved.

She relaxed finally and returned his gaze, not laughing now but with a bruised, quiet smile on her lips.

"Livie, we have a lot to talk about. Can we start to make plans now? Will you let me help you?"

Her smile turned to wariness in an instant. She turned away again. "I don't know. Please don't rush me."

Really? "You think I've been *rushing* you?"

"Rashid, please, there are things you don't know."

God, what would it take to earn her trust? "You're going to tell me the things I don't know, aren't you, Livie?" he demanded, trying to force confessions from her by sheer will.

Saddiq called from outside the tent. "Feramuz is

ready to take your car. Have you removed everything you need?"

"No, I'll be out in a second to unload it."

He said to Olivia, "You need to get packed. Do you need my help?"

"No, I can manage. But I don't really know what's happening."

"I'm sorry. I assumed Fatima told you. We're starting the trek today. We'll continue by horseback."

"Oh. What about your car?"

"I'm giving it to Saddiq. His cousin Feramuz is driving it back to Behruz City today, and another cousin is taking the jeep tomorrow."

"Oh, I see."

Rashid dressed and went out to unload the car.

****

When Olivia stepped into the sunlight she saw Rashid on the far side of the camp helping Saddiq take down the poles of his tent. He glanced her way briefly but then returned to his work. Fatima led her to one of the tents that was still standing.

After having breakfast with Jamal, she packed her things into saddlebags Fatima had given her and then went to watch the activity of the camp. She begged to be allowed to help, but her offer was rejected. She soon saw, as the nomads went about their tasks with the efficiency that comes from a lifetime of practice, that she wouldn't have been much help anyway. Keeping Jamal and the puppy out of the way of the workers turned out to be a fulltime job.

Rashid helped the men dismantle the tents and load everything onto the backs of donkeys and camels. Only when the work was done did he approach her.

His firm strides screamed his impatience. He wanted answers. And she wanted to give them to him. She wanted to give him everything, all that she was.

But Abu-Khan's threats and the fear he'd instilled in her paralyzed her.

Rashid lifted his hands toward her and then dropped them in a gesture of defeat. He could see her resistance. Her heart skidded, swelling with pain.

"We'll talk when we get to the new camp," he said.

Three men were trying to coax a heavily laden camel to rise from its kneeling position to its feet. The camel bellowed a wailing cry of self-pity and then complied.

"Yes," she said.

She was given a sweet-tempered horse named Amek, which meant "sky" in Qashami. Jamal sat in front of her, and the puppy rode in a basket tied behind her. Rashid and Saddiq stayed mostly at the rear of the caravan, but Rashid occasionally galloped ahead to join Olivia. He seemed to belong on a horse and on the high plateau. He looked primitive and strong and shatteringly masculine. Memories of their lovemaking tingled through her loins. She sat tall in the saddle, reveling in the sun on her face and the breeze in her hair, celebrating the return of her strength—her physical strength and the emotional strength that had been dormant while she lived under Abu-Khan's thumb. She was tired of holding back from Rashid, tired of denying what her heart knew. She wanted to move *forward* with her life—and *with Rashid*.

The other women and the older children walked. Younger children rode perched on top of the cargo on a donkey or camel while babies rested in shawls on their mothers' backs.

The new camp, which was high on a slope rising toward Gemdar Kuh, had a beautiful view stretching for miles toward mountains on the eastern horizon. Three other groups of nomads trudged slowly across the landscape with their herds.

After they'd eaten and set up their tent, Rashid asked her to go for a walk with him. Saddiq and Fatima volunteered to watch Jamal while they were gone.

She followed him along a small river that came down from the mountains above. He took her hand when the terrain became rough. That point of contact, her fingers laced with his, seemed to vibrate with the hum of sexual thirst that had not been quenched and questions that had not been answered.

They came to a place where the cliff was cut by a ravine and sat down on a large, flat rock.

Rashid waited. He said nothing.

"Okay," she said finally, as if he were forcing information from her by torture, "I'll tell you, but not until we get to Iran." She hadn't consciously decided, but her lips formed the words. Something in her had retreated from the stress of indecision, allowing her heart to decide. He deserved to know Jamal was his son. She would tell him.

"What?" His dark eyes bored into her. The breeze seemed to still. The world seemed to stop spinning. "What will you tell me, Livie?"

She was suddenly sure. "Everything. Whatever you want to know. When we've crossed over into Iran."

"Why wait?" he asked.

She told the truth. "Because I'll feel free of Abu-Khan when we're no longer in the country he rules."

But she didn't tell the whole truth. She didn't tell him he might hate her when he knew everything. She didn't know if he could forgive her. She wanted a little more time. And a few more nights like last night. That might be all she ever had of him.

"All right." He studied her face.

She repeated his words, "All right." She felt the calm certainty of resolve.

****

The smell of stew drew Rashid to the fire pit. He smelled lamb and some spice that brought back memories of his Behruzi grandmother's kitchen. Cardamom? Cumin? He'd never learned the names of the spices his grandmother used. She was gone now. She'd died a year before his father. He breathed in the familiar scents and the cool mountain air and relaxed now that Olivia had promised to tell him what was troubling her. She wouldn't go back on her word. He trusted that. When he knew the problem, he would be able to fix it. And then at last they could find their way to a future together.

They ate dinner by the fire pit. Olivia whispered questions and remarks about the food to Fatima, who sat next to her, but her conversation with Rashid was stilted and impersonal. Were he and Saddiq done with their work on the jeep? Yes, probably. They needed to test drive it. Was it likely to rain during the trek? No, the rainy season was over. Could he reach another piece of bread for Jamal, please? Yes, of course.

She must be thinking about the moment, only a few hours away now, when they would be in each other's arms again. They were sitting cross-legged on a rug near the fire. He inched toward her until their knees touched and then closer still so that their thighs were pressed together. Her face was flushed and her nostrils flared, but she didn't look at him. Still she returned the pressure against his thigh.

After dinner, Rashid went with Saddiq to test drive the jeep. When Saddiq declared the vehicle ready for the trip back to Behruz City, they returned to the camp.

"What's that?" Rashid asked Saddiq when they got back. Haunting music, like a violin but twangier and more Eastern, drifted through the mountain air like a siren's call. It screeched on nerves that were on fire already, waiting for the moment when he would close the tent flap and be alone with Livie.

"Oh, that will be Parshin playing his dotar," Saddiq replied.

Rashid followed the sound to the fire pit. A group of nomads stood in a circle around a turbaned old man sitting on a rug playing an instrument like the one Olivia had with her when she escaped the palace. Olivia was with the group. She was tapping her feet, swaying a little, responding, as she always did when there was music, *with movement.*

A tiny, gray-haired woman took Olivia's hand and pulled her into the center of the circle. The two began to dance, a sinuous, swaying dance with quick, small steps and broad arm movements. Olivia followed the old woman's lead, raising her slender arms over her head, sweeping them down and together, making graceful circles with her hands.

Fatima and two other women joined them, but Rashid never took his eyes from Olivia. She was so uninhibited, so attuned to the music, so free. She was a snake charmer, and he was the poor creature held in thrall by her movements.

But he would strike. Later tonight. She would move that lithe, enticing body against *him*. He would let her captivate him, and he would show her what *his body* could do when captivated.

Olivia spotted him among the other watchers. She smiled a seductive smile—*for him*—and kept dancing. *For him*. When the music ended, she came over to face him, moving still like a dancer, and asked breathlessly, "Can you get my dotar?"

He went to the car to get the instrument. The nomads watched and commented as she expertly adjusted the tautness of the strings. When she was ready, she had Saddiq ask the musician if she could play with him. The old man smiled a shy, toothless smile and bowed assent, and someone brought a rug for Olivia. She sat listening for a while and then joined in, harmonizing with the melody and adding little strums of rhythm now and then.

The rest of the camp had joined the circle. Everyone was quiet, even the children. Rashid stood spellbound.

No one spoke for a while after the song ended, then they all spoke at once.

"They want you to play an American song," Saddiq told Olivia.

"All right." She smiled at everyone. "I'll play the first song I learned on the piano when I was a child." She plucked a thin raspy melody, while the old man provided background chords to fill in. She sang in her sweet, clear voice.

Go tell Aunt Rhody, Go tell Aunt Rhody
Go tell Aunt Rhody

The old gray goose is dead

The nomads whispered questions to each other, and Saddiq whispered to Rashid, "I'm not sure I understood. What did the song say? Who died?" Rashid told him it was a goose that died.

"Oh." Saddiq chuckled. "That's what I thought she said." Saddiq translated the verse into Qashami for the others and they laughed.

"They think it's funny that the Americans have a song about a goose dying," he said.

Rashid and Olivia smiled at each other. Rashid smiled because the song was, indeed, silly and because the nomads' reaction to it was delightful and because he felt drunk with pleasure. Livie was going to reveal her secrets, and she would soon be in his arms again.

After each of the remaining verses of the song, Olivia and the old man strummed softly while Saddiq translated for the others.

She died in the mill pond, died in the mill pond,
She died in the mill pond
Standing on her head

When the song was over, everyone clamored for more.

"Okay," Olivia said. "This is a song about the freedom of living and riding in open country like this. It'll probably make more sense to you than the song about a dead goose." She strummed a more forceful beat and stronger melody and sang *Don't Fence Me In*.

She sang all three verses, repeating the chorus after each one and pausing for translation. The twangy sound of the dotar made a perfect accompaniment to the old cowboy song.

Everyone seemed awestruck. "They can't believe

the Americans have a song about *them*," Saddiq said.

"More, more, more" everyone cried. Olivia recognized the Qashami word for *more* without waiting for Saddiq's translation.

"Okay, one more. This song was written over a hundred years ago, and it's still popular at weddings today." The title is *Let Me Call You Sweetheart*. She started with a fast, cheerful beat, belying the message and not stopping for translation, but when she sang the chorus for the last time she slowed the pace. She sang to Rashid, twisting his heart with the promise of the words. The nomads were quiet, listening and watching the emotions flow between Rashid and Olivia.

Let me call you "Sweetheart," I'm in love with you.
Let me hear you whisper that you love me too.
Keep the love-light glowing in your eyes so true.
Let me call you "Sweetheart," I'm in love with you.

"I'm sorry you didn't get a chance to translate," Rashid told Saddiq when the song ended. "You can just tell them it's a song about love."

Saddiq laughed. "I think they could tell."

By the time everyone drifted away from the fire pit, stars were bright in the sky. A full moon in the east made the snow of Gemdar Kuh glow eerie above them. Nighttime sounds—the soft bleating of sheep, the clanging of camel bells, the distant hoot of an owl—replaced the dotar music. Olivia was still flushed from the music when she and Rashid slipped into their tent. Jamal had insisted on staying with Faroud again, so there would be just the two of them. Rashid lit the oil lamp and studied Olivia in its flickering light. She hadn't completely returned from that private world where music took her. She smiled and then slowly removed her clothes, preparing to bring their two worlds together.

When she was done, she stood before him, offering herself to his sight. Offering herself *to him*. He looked at her beautiful small breasts, at the smooth skin around her navel, at the puff of blonde hair below. He didn't deserve this pleasure, but he would take it. He would take everything she offered.

She lifted her arms as she had in the dance, sweeping them up and out and toward him. He was dizzy with wanting her. Her fingers skimmed across his chest, teasing open the buttons of his shirt. When it lay on the floor on top of her clothes, she reached for the drawstring that held the nomad pants and tugged at the tight bow. It wouldn't yield, so she tried picking at the knot.

"I could use some help here," she said.

He was enjoying the feel of her hands working where they were, tickling and tantalizing, but he couldn't wait any longer to be holding her. He took over the job and quickly stripped off the rest of his clothes.

They went into each other's arms and sank together onto the top of the sleeping bag. Their lovemaking was sweet, solemn, frenzied and wild. They touched and explored and kissed and sighed and moaned and kissed again, and joined their bodies and soared together to release.

And then they held each other and kissed and sighed some more.

Livie laid her head on his shoulder and stretched her arm across his chest, which swelled with love and a profound feeling of protectiveness. Her breathing became even and heavy. She was falling asleep.

"No, sweetheart, don't go to sleep on top of the bag."

She opened her eyes. Her lashes brushed his chest. They rolled and shifted and laughed and dealt with zippers until they were warm and covered and her head was on his shoulder again. She went to sleep, while Rashid held her, feeling powerful and protective, thinking about how magnificent she had been, dancing and singing, charming everyone with her talent and her sweetness. And giving herself to him.

Would he ever hear her whisper the words of the song: that she *loved him too*? Perhaps when she revealed her secrets she would be ready to say it.

The next day she asked Rashid to take Jamal and the puppy so she could walk instead of riding the horse.

"Are you sure you're strong enough?"

"Yes. I don't want to be set apart from the other women."

Rashid kept his eyes on her for the rest of the day and the days that followed. His heart monitored her movements as faithfully as a compass points to the north. Her beauty as she strode up the grassy slope in her bright costume made his heart swell with love and pride. Even when he was too far away to hear, he could imagine the music her ankle bracelets made when she moved.

He wasn't normally a patient man, but he found a new capacity for patience while he waited for Olivia's confession, or whatever it was going to be. At last he had peace from all the speculations that had been torturing him. She was going to tell. He wasn't afraid of what she would reveal. Nothing she could say would change the way he felt. He loved her. He worshipped her. There was no obstacle too big for him to overcome. He would beat down every objection, every fear, every doubt. He was utterly sure. That was why he could wait.

Waiting became his sacred ritual. He loved breathing the mountain air. He loved seeing her among the other women, taller than the rest, straighter, more graceful, and so unaware of her beauty. He loved the nights, when she became a siren, an enchantress, a courtesan.

He was still nervous about the border crossing. There would be soldiers in the pass, but they would be on the alert for rebel activity, not nomad migrations. Soon they would be in Iran. Then she would tell him.

Their lovemaking on the last night in Behruz was like a sacrament. Olivia was all fluid movement. Her gentle, graceful hands swept across his face, his shoulders, his back, his hips, his belly, his groin. She slid her feet up and down the length of his legs and then shifted her own legs between his, twisting and twining, arching against him, all the while kissing him and drinking in his kisses. He lay still while she moved against him, patient even in this, until finally they joined together and moved together. And climaxed together. And then they clung to each other and drifted into peaceful sleep.

****

Olivia loved walking with the other women. She wanted to be one of them. She loved their earthiness. She loved her own earthiness. She took long strides, feeling womanly and sensual and strong. They were at the edge of a grassy plateau now, with steep rocky slopes rising to tall mountains on either side.

Their progress was slow because patches of grass along the edge of the trail enticed the animals to graze. It was a charmed place kept green by water from the melting snow above. She was spellbound. There were tiny purple flowers growing out of crevices between the rocks and then, farther on, large bushes covered in clusters of pink trumpet flowers, just a few bushes at first but then more as they continued into the valley. It was like a fairyland.

"What are the flowers?" she asked Rashid when he came near on his horse.

"Wild rhododendrons. They're native to the area."

They would soon be in Iran. It was fitting that the place that marked her departure from Behruz and from Abu-Khan's control seemed to be the most enchanted place on earth.

When they saw Behruzi soldiers ahead, Rashid handed the puppy to Jamal, whose head had been freshly shaved for the occasion, and had Olivia get behind him on the horse. Saddiq chatted with the soldiers while the rest of the caravan shuffled past. Rashid stayed at the far edge of the caravan, placing the entire herd of sheep between them and the soldiers. Olivia, with her hair hidden under her mantle, held fast to Rashid, her whole upper body plastered against his back and her face turned away from the soldiers.

Half an hour later they spotted Iranian soldiers and once again Rashid rode on the far side of the animals.

The soldiers stopped Saddiq and talked to him for a few minutes, and they made a desultory search of the cargo on two of the camels. "They're looking for drugs and weapons," Rashid told her. "They're not interested in pretty Americans escaping from Behruz."

When they'd proceeded out of sight of the soldiers, Rashid said quietly, "We're in Iran."

He hadn't mentioned her confession, not once since she'd promised to make it, but now it appeared his patience was at an end.

"When we reach camp," she said. She stayed on the horse for the rest of the trip, clinging to Rashid, clinging to hope and praying. *Please let him understand. Let him forgive. Let this be the beginning of our life as a family.*

After about an hour, they stopped on a wide grassy slope facing west over Iran's immense eastern desert. The nomads went to work setting up the camp that would be their permanent home for the summer. The grass would be watered by melting snow from Gemdar Kuh and by underground springs. When the rains began again in the fall, they would return to their winter grazing land in Behruz.

As soon as he'd set up their tent, Rashid asked Fatima if she would watch Jamal for a while, saying simply, "I need to talk to Olivia."

The time had come. With her heart thudding like a jackhammer, she followed him to the tent.

Chapter Eleven

Now. She would tell him. He'd felt confident he could solve whatever problem she might reveal to him, but suddenly he was nervous. What if it was too big or somehow beyond his power to fix?

He was so tired of speculating.

He opened the flap and stood aside while she entered. Then he followed her inside and closed it. She sat down cross-legged on the rug and waited while he lit the lantern. Then he sat facing her. He waited. She was fidgeting with the zipper pull on her sleeping bag.

"I'm waiting, Livie." He was ready to snap, but he tried to sound encouraging.

She continued her work on the zipper. "Before I start, you have to promise you won't go rushing off to Behruz City. You must never discuss anything I'm about to tell you with Abu-Khan."

"Okay."

"You have to promise, Rashid. Say the words. Say that you promise."

"All right. I promise I will never discuss anything you're about to tell me with Abu-Khan."

"Thank you."

"First of all, I want you to know that I didn't abandon you two years ago. I thought you had abandoned me."

What? That was impossible. "I tried to call you a

dozen times. You were never available. And then one of the secretaries explained that you didn't want to talk to me."

"When did you first call?" she asked.

"I don't remember. Not right away. I was practically sequestered when I was in Washington. The talks were all top secret, and there were endless meetings. I called when I got back to California. It was probably about two weeks after I left Behruz."

"I tried to call you too. That is, I had one of the secretaries place calls to you. He kept telling me he couldn't reach you. And then..." Tears threatened to spill from her eyes. He wanted to reach for her, hold her, help her get through this, but he was frozen, hardly breathing, waiting to see what else she would say. "Abu-Khan made it sound like your wedding was imminent."

Rashid took her hand. "Oh Livie, no. I couldn't marry Shamsi, not after what you and I shared, not feeling about you as I did. I broke it off with her as soon as I got back to California."

"Well, the impression I got was the exact opposite."

"Livie, darling, how could you have thought I didn't care? I loved you with my life."

"I don't know. I'd always looked up to you so much. I hardly dared believe you could love me."

If Abu-Khan's damned secretaries had kept him from reaching Olivia, they had done it at Abu-Khan's request. But why? It didn't make sense. "But there was your letter."

"What letter?" she asked.

"The letter you wrote to me. Don't tell me you

didn't write it, Livie, because I know your handwriting. It said that if I ever tried to touch you again you would leave Behruz and never come back. It said you would tell your sister."

Olivia gasped. She went pale.

"What?"

"I did write that letter, Rashid, but not to you. It didn't have your name on it, did it?"

"I don't remember. I didn't notice. The envelope was addressed to me, and the letter was signed by you. What was I supposed to think?"

"I wrote it to Abu-Khan when I was fifteen years old. I never dreamed he would have *saved* it."

"To Abu-Khan? When you were fifteen? My God, Livie, what did he do?" His grip on her hand tightened. Fear and dread were acid in his heart.

"It doesn't matter now. He touched me. He tried to…well…you know, but I stopped him before he did anything too serious. He never tried anything again."

No, no, no, not his sweet Livie. She'd had to face that alone. "Livie, you should have told Karen. You should have told *me*. I would have gotten you away from there. You could have stayed with my mother."

She was studying the bottom of the tent flap. "I'm not sure Karen would have believed me. She certainly wouldn't have wanted to know. And you were in the U.S. when it happened. I don't think I would have told you even if you had been in Behruz. I felt dirty and ashamed, as if it were my fault. Anyway, I kept my distance from him after that, and by the time I saw you again I was pretty sure he wasn't going to try it again."

"How could you keep coming back after that? Why did you stay after Karen was gone?"

"I had to stay. Jamal needed me."

Still she refused to look at him.

He tried to calm his voice. He tried to sound gentle. "Is there more?" He took her other hand.

Her hands were shaking.

"Tell me, Livie."

She spoke in a hoarse whisper. "Jamal is not Abu-Khan's son." He leaned toward her to hear her softly spoken words. "Karen was not his real mother. They adopted him. They pretended to be his natural parents because Abu-Khan needed an heir, but Abu-Khan didn't love him. He never loved him. Not like I did."

Then he knew. He closed his eyes against the knowledge, but he knew. He'd been ready to save Olivia from some outside threat, but what would he do if her problems were *her own fault*? How could he help her if she'd done something he could never forgive? He knew already, but she had to say it. "Who are Jamal's real parents?"

"We are. I am his mother. You are his father."

He was silent. He released her hands. "My son. Jamal is my son. Why didn't you tell me? Why did you give him away?"

He rose to his feet. He loomed over her. It was an intimidating stance, he knew. He wanted to intimidate. "Why, Livie?"

She shifted her gaze from the tent flap to his feet. She spoke slowly, without emotion, almost as if it had happened to someone else. She'd been despondent, pregnant, suffering morning sickness, and alone. She'd thought Rashid didn't want her. Abu-Khan and Karen had been relentless in their attempts to persuade her, and in the end, they won. She told him how she and

Karen had hidden in the Summer Palace during much of her pregnancy so Abu-Khan would be able to claim the baby had been born to his wife and how Abu-Khan had threatened to keep Jamal from her if she ever revealed the truth.

She recounted that last interview when Abu-Khan said he wanted to marry her.

After telling him everything, all in that monotone whisper, she stood up to face him. "Please understand."

His mind reeled—with sorrow for what she'd suffered, and with fury because she'd made that decision without him.

"You do see why I made you promise not to talk to Abu-Khan, don't you?" she asked. "He would do anything to keep us apart. He's dangerous, Rashid. Please don't forget it."

He wanted to strangle her. And he wanted to strangle Abu-Khan for hurting her!

"So what are you going to do? Are you going back to Behruz?"

"No! No I can't, not now. I'll live in the States with Jamal. I'll have to hide. I'll have to use an assumed name. Abu-Khan will never stop looking for me."

"I see. And what about me? Do I have any place in your plans?"

"I don't know. It doesn't seem possible. But we can talk about it, can't we?"

"Yes. We most certainly will be talking about it."

"Please don't be angry. I wanted to tell you. I was just so afraid of Abu-Khan. You don't really know him. I was afraid for your safety as well as mine."

"Oh, I see, you kept this information from me *for my own good*? You might have trusted me to make my own decisions about that."

"Well maybe, but... Oh, Rashid, you can't understand. You don't know what it's like to be afraid."

"I think I do, Livie. I was there when you were injured during the explosion, remember? I caught you when you fell, and I felt your blood soaking through my shirt when I carried you to safety. I know about fear, Livie, believe me."

"I'm so sorry. I do appreciate all you've done for me."

He interrupted her. "Oh that's nice. I have your *appreciation*."

"I'm sorry I didn't tell you sooner."

"Well, I guess I should *appreciate* that you've told me now. But you'll have to excuse me. I would like to see my son." He slipped through the opening of the tent, his mind numb to the suffering he'd heard in Olivia's voice. The pain she felt now was pain she'd brought on herself. Because she hadn't trusted him.

Jamal sat in the dirt on the other side of the fire pit with two other children, playing with their cars. His son. *His and Olivia's son*. His heart was so full of hurt and betrayal and love, it seemed it would burst.

Jamal was his son.

****

Feeling dazed as if she'd been beaten, Olivia followed Rashid outside.

He was standing near the fire pit several feet from the boys, apparently timid about approaching. Olivia watched him watch their son, her heart choked with love for both of them. She had dreamed of sharing this moment with Rashid, this moment when he looked at their beautiful son with the loving eyes of a father, but he wouldn't let her share it. And she could see why. What if someone had robbed her of the first fourteen months of Jamal's life? Would she forgive? No, it was an unpardonable crime.

After a while, Rashid approached the group and sat down in the dirt to join their play. Soon he was helping them build a ramp of rocks and dirt for the cars.

Olivia stayed in front of the tent, looking out over the broad sweep of valley, stealing occasional glances at the little group. The nomads, busy setting up camp, didn't seem to notice her or the man and children playing with cars.

Rashid didn't acknowledge her presence, but a desire to punish her radiated from him. The tenderness on his face was for Jamal, not for her. He might never forgive her. She'd tried to prepare herself for such a reaction, but her heart had always clung to the fantasy that he would understand and would love her for being the mother of his child.

He ignored her all afternoon, helping the men with their work while Olivia attempted to help the women prepare the meal. She sat on a mat in the corner of Saddiq's tent, shelling pistachio nuts. It took about twice as long as it had taken Saddiq's ten-year-old daughter to do the same job the previous night, but the nomad women made a big show of admiring her effort.

Rashid sat next to her during the evening meal with Jamal on his lap. Somehow, he managed to avoid touching her, and he directed his remarks to everyone but her. Rejection emanated from him like a cloud of ice crystals, but no one seemed to notice.

When they were done eating, she went with a few of the other women to a stream to wash her underwear and a few of Jamal's pants and shirts. She would have washed Rashid's clothes too, but she didn't want to rummage through his things and she didn't want to approach him, not while he was so pointedly ignoring her.

Back in the camp, she took a nap with Jamal and the puppy. When they came out afterward, she saw Rashid with Saddiq at the far side of the camp, their heads together, talking intently. She stared at him, daring him to ignore her once again, and this time he returned her gaze. A glint of speculation in his eyes worried her.

Jamal had set out toddling across the camp toward the two men, the puppy at his feet. Only when he reached them did Rashid turn his attention from Olivia. He picked up the boy settled him on his arm, and kissed him on the forehead. Then, after speaking a few more words to Saddiq, he approached Olivia.

"Thank you," he said. "Thank you for giving me such a beautiful son. Thank you for telling me."

"You had a right to know. I'm sorry I didn't tell you sooner."

"He has my father's eyes, you know."

"No, Rashid, he has *your* eyes. That day when you first met him I thought it was possible that you might notice the resemblance."

"Oh, no, I couldn't have. I never suspected a thing. He could have been a carbon copy of me and I wouldn't have seen it. It never occurred to me. Well, of course it did two years ago, after we made love. When I came back to Behruz a few months later, I was wondering. I knew it could have happened and I actually hoped it had, because then you would have had to establish some kind of relationship with me. At least that's what I thought. I never imagined you'd give my child away."

"Please Rashid, don't make it sound like that. I was desolate. I was almost crazy those first few months. I didn't know what I was doing, and Abu-Khan and Karen were so persuasive."

"Yes, I can imagine they were. But if you'd only *trusted* me…"

Tired of listening to adult conversation, Jamal squirmed to get down. "Puppy?" he asked when Rashid set him on the ground. They looked around, but the puppy had disappeared.

"Wait a minute," Rashid said to Jamal. "I'll help you find the puppy as soon as I'm done talking to Olivia…that is, *to your mommy*."

Her heart leaped when she heard those words, *your mommy*, and her cheeks blazed. Would she ever feel she had a right to the simple pleasure of being called *Mommy*?

Her reaction brought a shadow to Rashid's face. "Tell me, Olivia, do you feel fully recovered?"

"Yes." She was surprised by his sudden change of topic. "I'm fine. Why are you asking?"

"Just don't overdo it. Ask for help if you need it. If I'm not around, ask Saddiq or Fatima."

"Don't worry, Rashid. Everyone has been very kind. I don't need any special pampering."

"Okay. Well, I'm going to help find the puppy." He headed in the direction of the animals, leaving Olivia standing by the tent. *What was that about? What was he planning?*

The puppy was found trying to befriend one of the huge nomad dogs and was given yet another bone to gnaw while they ate with the others around a fire in the center of the camp. Rashid held Jamal in his lap and sat next to Olivia, but he didn't touch her. His attention seemed to wander, and twice Saddiq had to repeat a question he'd asked him.

It was taken for granted that Jamal would sleep with Faroud in Saddiq's tent once again, not that it mattered to Olivia. There wouldn't be a return of intimacy with Rashid, not after he'd ignored her most of the day. He wouldn't want it, and she wouldn't permit it.

Rashid stayed by the fire while Olivia settled Jamal in Saddiq's tent. Once in her own tent, she changed into Rashid's shirt, separated the sleeping bags, and slid into hers, hoping to fall asleep before Rashid arrived.

But it was only minutes later that she heard the opening of the flap. She lay on her side facing the wall of the tent, breathing slowly to simulate sleep.

He said, "I know you're awake."

She continued her slow breathing and waited, hoping… Hoping what? That he would leave? That he would stay? That he would ignore her or that he would make love to her? There was silence. He must be watching her, waiting for her to give a sign that she was awake. Well, she could outwait him. She sighed, mimicking the sound Jamal made when he was sleeping. Then she heard the sound of the zipper of Rashid's bag, a long rasp as he pulled it down. Another silence followed. She thought he'd stretched out, but he hadn't. He'd moved to her side. His hands fumbled with the zipper at her back.

She kept her eyes closed, willing him to leave her alone. It seemed like the ultimate test of her pride that she refuse to acknowledge him. Damn him. He couldn't blame and ignore her all day and then expect her to welcome him into her arms at night.

Cool air wafted between her shoulder blades and brushed along her spine as he slowly opened the zipper. She was curled up, leaving the bottom half of the bag empty, but he pulled the zipper all the way down to the lower corner and across the bottom.

"I know you're awake," he said again.

When she didn't acknowledge him, he moved from the foot of the sleeping bag back up beside her, and then cool air whooshed over her whole body. He'd thrown open the bag, leaving her uncovered, wearing nothing but the thin shirt and her briefs.

She didn't move. His hand touched her shoulder and she stiffened, resisting him. It slid along her collarbone and then down to brush the swell of her breast.

She pushed his hand away from her. "Leave me alone!" She scrambled onto her knees to face him, ready to strike if he tried to touch her again. *How dare he judge her!* Anger became strength, an old strength reawakened. It filled her with confidence and resolve. Abu-Khan's domination had weakened her, made her too easy to intimidate. But that was over. She was tired of the domination of *men*!

"Leave me alone! I don't want you. Go away!"

He held his hands up in surrender, his expression innocent and full of questions. His chest was bare, but he was still wearing his pants. He extended his hands toward her, palms up in appeal, but she slammed her own hands down on his arms, pushing him away.

Where did this rage come from? The suddenness

and vehemence of it shocked her as much as it must have shocked him. She struck his arms again, with all her strength, furious with him for two long years long years of suffering and for his blaming reaction when she told him the truth. She hit at his upper arms and his chest with her clenched fists. He tried to catch her wrists, to stop her, but she lurched away. He was talking to her, saying her name, trying to calm her, but she was in the grip of a fury that could not hear reason. She continued to lash at him, using all her strength.

"Don't, Livie, please don't do this. You'll hurt yourself." He reached for her again, ignoring her blows, but she pushed at his chest and he dropped his hands.

Anger twisted in her, a biting pain in her belly, anger at Abu-Khan, at Rashid, and at all men. A wolf howled in the distance and the nomad dogs howled their response. The sheep became quiet. Rashid's voice whispered through the tent. "Don't fight me, Livie. I can't stand to see you like this. Can you tell me what this is about?"

"You know," she said in a tight monotone, unable to put the hurt and anger of two long years into words.

"Maybe I do know, or at least I can imagine, but you have to tell me. Come on, say it."

"No. Just leave me alone."

His muscular chest and arms dominated the small space. His eyes, wounded and worried, accused her. What could she say? How could she explain? She didn't even know herself where this explosion of hurt and anger had come from.

"Say it, Livie. Why are you so angry?"

What he meant, she was sure, was *why was she so angry when* he *was the one who'd been wronged*? He

174

didn't say the words, but she heard them and anger flared even hotter.

"Because…" She gestured vaguely at his naked chest. Tears streamed down her face, but she ignored them. "Because of all your judging, blaming superiority. You don't know what it was like when you left. You don't know anything. You think just because you didn't know about Jamal, just because you came back and tried to find me *once*, that you're blameless, but Abu-Khan took advantage of me when I was vulnerable and alone, and *you weren't here*. I paid for my mistake every day for two long years and *you weren't here*. You don't know anything. You have no right to blame me. I can *never* forgive you for not being here."

"I'm sorry, Livie, I'm so sorry."

She heard the suffering in his voice. As soon as she'd spoken the words, *I can never forgive you*, she knew they were no longer true. Expressing her anger and pain had been the only thing standing between her and forgiveness. She felt empty and drained. Rashid pulled her onto his lap and kissed her tear-drenched face, and she collapsed against him. She rested her head on his shoulder and felt *peace*.

He held her for a long time, and then he pulled back a little and kissed her forehead. Strands of her hair were stuck in the moisture of sweat and tears on her face. He smoothed the strands away and then shifted her onto the bag beside him. They stretched out on their sides facing each other, breathing quietly, gazing at each other.

What had happened? Had all that pain and anger actually been festering in her heart? It was gone. It had burst from her in that terrible outpouring of emotion and then had simply vanished. By expressing it so violently she'd used it up. She was cleansed; she'd set down a terrible burden. She was full of love and a great sense of peace and rightness. She was where she belonged, beside Rashid.

Camel bells clanged, and sheep bleated. A baby cried in a nearby tent.

Desire built slowly in Rashid's eyes. He didn't move. Her body responded with a rush of need that had been there all along, part of the anger. Rashid slowly unbuttoned her shirt, his lips pursed in concentration. When he was done, she removed the shirt and her briefs while he rolled away to shed his own clothes and find a foil packet. Finally they lay naked, facing each other again, their breathing no longer slow and easy. She was weak from her outburst; she could scarcely move. But lust pumped like syrup through her veins.

He touched her cheek, her mouth, her chin, and then his hand slid down her neck to her shoulder and to her breast. His knuckles skimmed across one nipple and then the other, sparking a fire that jolted her out of her lethargy. She jerked and arched toward him, wrapping her arms around his neck. She rolled onto her back and pulled him against her.

He moaned her name. "You want this?"

She murmured *yes*.

He waited, poised above her. She parted her legs and arched toward him, wild with need, and then he filled her with the power of his own need. His mouth came down to hers and he kissed her while they moved together, unhurried, then paused and let the passion build, until pleasure was almost pain, but it was beautiful too, and then they couldn't pause any more, and there was an explosion of feeling so intense her heart seemed to stop.

He collapsed on top of her with all his weight, and then, when she murmured a protest, he slid a little to the side. They were bathed in sweat and tears, and her hair was once again plastered against her forehead. She was hot, and his skin burned where it covered her.

His breathing relaxed and then drifted into the slow, smooth sighing sounds of sleep.

She slept too but woke some time later, chilled by the cold night air, aware that Rashid was no longer beside her. He was moving in the tent, spreading the second sleeping bag over her. When he slid back into the warmth beside her, he took her into his arms and kissed her softly on her raw, swollen lips. Soon he was asleep again.

But Olivia couldn't sleep. Her mind was in a fever of resolve. How could she have let Abu-Khan intimidate her for so long? She should have confronted him long ago. She wanted to confront him now. She knew what she would say, and she wanted to say it. She had to say it. If only she could be transported back to Behruz for just an hour, she could have the satisfaction of facing Abu-Khan from the strength she now felt instead of from the weakness he had imposed on her. The weakness she had *let* him impose on her.

Thoughts raced through her mind, demanding expression. She reached for the flashlight and inched away from the beloved form sleeping beside her to find paper and a pen in her saddlebag. She sat beside Rashid in the small tent that had sheltered their passion, the quiet of the mountain night broken only by the bleating of sheep, and she wrote words her heart had been screaming to say ever since Karen's death.

Abu-Khan,

I am gone. I have left your country and I am not coming back. Jamal is with me, and we are with Rashid. We are a family; we belong together. I think you know that. Don't try to find us. I'm sorry, Abu-Khan. I'm sorry you lost Karen; I'm sorry Jamal cannot fill your need for an heir. I wish you happiness. Goodbye.

Goodbye goodbye goodbye. Why hadn't she been able to say these words before? She'd needed to get away from Abu-Khan's influence to remember her strength. She'd needed to feel loved to reclaim the power love gave. She felt free. Of Abu-Khan, of resentment, of pain and fear. She *was* free. The future seemed dazzling bright and full of promise.

She set the paper and pen aside, turned off the flashlight, and slid down into the sleeping bag, backing up against the wall of Rashid's chest. His arm came around her, and she sighed, barely able to contain her happiness. Should she wake him? She needed to tell him that somehow her flood of anger and passion had cleansed away all the pain of the last two years. The last words she spoke to him, *I will never forgive you*, were not true. There was nothing to forgive. It was over.

His breath touched her cheek; his arm tightened around her. She would tell him tomorrow. Soon she was asleep too.

Chapter Twelve

She awoke slowly the next morning, stretching out her arm, reaching for the comfort of Rashid, but he wasn't there. He must be outside helping the men set up camp. She should get up. She should be watching Jamal. But a beautiful, drowsy inertia made her slide back down into the warmth of the sleeping bag for a few minutes more of laziness.

An aching weakness in her muscles and bruised soreness everywhere reminded her how roughly and passionately she'd used her body last night. She brushed her hands across her breasts, feeling their tenderness, remembering Rashid's hands on them. And his mouth. How amazing it was that her eruption of anger and the release she'd experienced in his arms had healed the angry pain she'd kept buried for so long. She couldn't wait to see him. She'd said such hateful things. She had to tell him the pain and anger were gone.

She reached over to the corner of the tent where she'd left her clothes, but then she froze with her arm outstretched. There was a piece of paper on top of the pile of clothes, folded and with her name on it, written in Rashid's careful handwriting.

She reached for the paper and slowly opened it. Dread clogged her throat, but a tiny splinter of hope said maybe she was wrong.

Olivia,

I'm sorry about the promise. It was too much to ask. I have to see Abu-Khan. Saddiq will take care of you.

Rashid

No. She pulled on her clothes, not bothering with the petticoats, and ran from the tent, searching desperately for Rashid. He was nowhere in sight, but she found Saddiq working with the other men gathering rocks for a fire pit.

"Where is Rashid?" She prayed it was not too late.

"He's gone back to Behruz City. I thought he told you. He said he has some important business with the sultan."

No. Oh God, please no.

"When did he leave? How long ago?"

"About three hours."

"We must stop him, Saddiq. Please help me. Can someone ride after him? Can I?"

"No, he took our fastest horse, and he has a good head start. But don't worry. We'll take good care of you and the child. I promised Rashid we would. You'll be with him soon; you'll see. He'll meet you in Tehran. He'll fly there from Behruz City."

"Do you have a cell phone? Can we call him?"

"No, I'm sorry, that is not possible. I won't have service until I get to an Iranian city to arrange it, and Rashid won't have a signal until he gets back to Behruz City. But really, khanoum, you need not worry. You will be together soon."

Olivia thought about how irrational and obsessed Abu-Khan had been the last time she saw him. He could kill Rashid; he was capable of it.

But Rashid didn't know that.

"How will he make it through the pass?" she asked. "Won't the soldiers stop him?"

"He'll cross the border on the main road this time, through the official crossing. He's using my passport in case the guards are watching for him."

"Through the official crossing? On horseback?"

Saddiq laughed. "No. He rode to the Iranian city of Birjand, about two hours west of here. I have relatives there. He'll pay them to drive him to Behruz City and bring the horse back up here."

She looked out over the broad plain, trying to spot a lone horseman, willing Rashid to come back, but the only movement she saw came from vultures cruising low, searching for prey.

"When did he decide to make this trip?" Had he decided this morning? Had she forced him away with the harsh words she spoke last night?

"He discussed it with me yesterday. He asked me to take you to Birjand. You can fly to Tehran from there. Rashid gave me money for you. Mamad, a friend who was at UCLA with us, will help you in Tehran."

Of course it had all been carefully planned, and it had probably been decided from the moment he found out Jamal was his son. He would be thinking of himself as the great hero, confronting Abu-Khan, reasoning with him, and convincing him to give up his claim to Jamal. If only it were that simple!

Trust me, he'd said.

Promise me you won't go to Behruz, she'd said.

I promise, he'd said.

And then he'd gone.

Stupid, arrogant, chauvinistic asshole!

Asshole, jerk, bully, prick!

Prick!

Saddiq returned to his work, and Olivia stood watching the vultures, her last words to Rashid echoing in her mind. *I can never forgive you.* Forgiveness was no longer the issue. Now she knew she could never *trust* him again.

Worry for his safety, fear about her own future, love, and resentment, all swirled in her mind, and adrenalin surged as she prepared to leave with Saddiq for her own trip by horse to Birjand.

The letter she'd written last night was gone. Rashid must have found it. She hoped he was taking it to Abu-Khan. She didn't regret writing it; she wanted Abu-Khan to see it.

She found the puppy and gave him his second pill. It must have been about two weeks since he got the first one, even though it felt like a lifetime.

****

Rashid rode away from the camp like a knight on his charger. He would be the hero. He would deserve Olivia's love.

Anticipation of her gratitude and her love spurred him on as he travelled toward the border with Saddiq's brother-in-law, but when they were back in Behruz, making their way through the barren western plain, he began to have doubts. Her words haunted him.

You have to promise.

Say the words.

He remembered the urgency on her face when she demanded that promise.

And he remembered his own words. *Trust me.*

How could she trust him now? What had he done? She was a grown woman, a liberated, smart, *American* woman who was used to solving her own problems.

His own upbringing had given him a mixed message in that regard, and the prejudice he'd experienced in America had left him feeling he had something to prove. But Olivia never made him feel that way. She never demanded heroic gestures or implied he had to *win* her love by saving her.

She did love him. She'd shown him that in every way a woman could. If he lost her now, it wouldn't be because he was a Middle Easterner and she was a golden goddess. It would be because he hadn't earned her trust.

But her plan to live a life in hiding was ridiculous.

And he was sure he could make Abu-Khan see reason.

He would call her. As soon as he came within range of the cell phone towers of Behruz City he would call. He would explain, and she would understand. *Hopefully* she would understand.

Their progress was agonizingly slow. The speedometer said they were going fifty miles an hour. Couldn't they go faster?

He shouldn't have left her. He was heading toward an action that would be a betrayal she might never forgive. But he needed to confront Abu-Khan. For her.

He checked his cell phone every few minutes for the rest of the trip, but there was never a signal. They reached Behruz City. Still no signal. Saddiq's brother-in-law took him to Reza's house. Still no signal.

"The rebels have taken over the cell phone towers," Reza explained.

"Do you have a landline?"

Reza didn't, and he didn't know anyone who did.

He explained that almost no one in Behruz had had phone service before the cell phone towers were built.

Rashid felt like crying. Why had he come back? He needed to be with Olivia.

****

The city of Tehran, with its tall buildings, its billboards, and its bright lights, made Behruz seem like a place out of the Middle Ages. Olivia felt like a country bumpkin gazing at the sights as Saddiq's uncle drove her on modern freeways and crowded streets to the home of Rashid's friend Mamad in the northern part of the city. Mamad introduced her to his wife Soosi, and their son Baasha, who was two years older than Jamal, and then told her how relieved they were to see her. They'd been expecting her for three days. He'd been waiting for a call asking him to pick her up at the airport.

He'd heard from Rashid. It wasn't easy to place calls from Behruz—apparently the rebels had found a way to interrupt cell phone signals—but Rashid had gotten through to Mamad twice.

"What did he say? Is he okay? Has he reached Behruz City? Has he seen Abu-Khan?"

Mamad laughed. "He didn't tell me a thing about what's going on; the entire conversation was about you. He was worried because you hadn't arrived yet."

She was awakened on her first morning in Mamad's house by a servant girl who handed her a cell phone. Olivia's hand shook as she drew the phone to her ear. Her heart clenched. She whispered *hello* in a quaking voice.

"Hello Livie. God, where have you been? I've been worried sick about you."

Anger eclipsed all her other feelings. "Where have *I* been? *You've* been worried about *me*?"

"Yes. You were supposed to arrive in Tehran three days ago. What happened?"

"Well it turns out you can't just get on an Iranian plane with a puppy in your arms. There's a lot of paperwork involved. The puppy needs shots and a certificate from a veterinarian."

Rashid mumbled a profanity in Farsi.

Ha! One of his oh-so-carefully-laid-out plans had a flaw! That little triumph was almost worth the discomfort of the twenty-hour trip by car with Saddiq's cigar-smoking uncle.

"How did you get to Tehran?" he asked.

"Never mind, Rashid. I figured it out. I'm here. The question is: where are you? Have you seen Abu-Khan?"

"I'm in Behruz City. I believe I'll be allowed to see him tomorrow."

"Well, good luck with that. I'm sure you don't need any input from me."

"Olivia, I'm sorry about the promise."

"No, Rashid, I don't want to hear your apologies. You can't get away with breaking a promise that easily."

"So you're mad at me."

"Yes, Rashid, I'm mad at you. The word *mad* hardly covers how I feel."

"Okay, you're right. I realized that before I got here. I'm really, truly sorry. I was wrong to break the promise. I was wrong to think I knew better than you how to handle this."

"And yet there you are, in Behruz City, about to do

exactly what you promised not to do."

"I won't see Abu-Khan if you don't want me to. I'll leave for Tehran as soon as I can. It may take a while. The airport is closed and I believe the border is about to be closed too, but I'll come back to you without seeing him if that's what you want. It's up to you."

"Really?"

"Yes, really. I was wrong. Whatever you think of me, whatever names you've called me, I've called myself worse."

Olivia smiled a quiet little private smile. "I doubt that. I called you an *asshole* and a *prick*."

"You called me a *prick*?"

"Yes."

"Well, you're right. I wouldn't have thought of that. I was thinking more in the line of *chauvinist* and *barbarian*."

"*Barbarian*. I like that. I'll use it next time."

"I hope you won't need to use any of those words ever again, Livie. I'm going to listen to you. Really. I want to learn to deserve your trust."

"You know you were wrong?"

"Yes!" He yelled his exasperation.

She smiled, this time a wide, exultant smile. She smiled tenderly at Jamal, who was asleep in the crib Mamad had set up beside her bed. In spite of all her fear and anger, she smiled. Rashid had said the one thing he needed to say to make forgiveness possible. *He knew he'd been wrong.*

He sighed. "Listen, Livie, you can gloat all day after we hang up, but now you have to decide what you want me to do. Do you want me to give Abu-Khan your letter?"

"I do want him to have my letter, but will you be safe?"

"Can you please trust me in this one matter, Livie? I know my uncle. He won't harm me."

"You'll need to flatter him," she said at the same time as Rashid said, "I'll have to flatter him."

They laughed. Their laughter zinged back and forth through the airways between Behuz City and Tehran.

"What can I possibly say to flatter him now when I think he's the lowest life form ever to walk on the earth?"

"You can do this, Rashid. Start with sympathy. Start with *poor Abu-Khan.* Talk about his dedication to his people and about how ungrateful they are."

"Yes, he'll be feeling martyred."

"I've been thinking… If Abu-Khan decides to fight me for Jamal, if he goes to court with the adoption paper, then the whole world will know he did *not* sire a son and he lied to make everyone believe he had. Surely his male vanity will keep him from letting that happen.

"You're right. Should I use that? Should I threaten to expose him?"

"You won't have to. He'll have thought of it. His bullying me was a bluff. You need to help him save face as much as possible."

"So you want me to see him?"

"Yes, but this doesn't make it all right for you to have gone against my wishes."

"Yes, I know that."

"Be careful."

"I will."

"Call me as soon as you've seen him."

"I will."

I love you. She didn't say the words. She was still angry, but she was full of hope too. They would find their way back to trust.

If he could get out of Behruz alive. If he could return safely to her arms.

That afternoon, Mamad took her to visit the Swiss embassy, the airline, a veterinarian, and various businesses that could help make the arrangements for them to leave Iran once Rashid had joined them. Modern young women in Tehran just covered their hair with scarves, but older women still wore chador*s*, and Olivia did too. She wanted anonymity.

Every time Mamad's cell phone rang, Olivia's heart took up its familiar place in her throat, but it was always business for Mamad. When he had to go to work on her second day there, he got a cell phone for Olivia and told her he'd give the number to Rashid when he called.

But no call came. Olivia spent most of the day in the courtyard listening to the BBC on the radio while Jamal and Baasha splashed in a wading pool nearby. The puppy ran circles around the pool trying to be part of the fun without getting wet.

At noon she heard that the cell phone towers in Behruz had been destroyed. So there would be no call. The same towers were used to relay internet signals. There would be no email.

At three o'clock, she heard there'd been an attack on the old fortress. The BBC journalist announced "The sultan of Behruz and his son are both believed to be dead."

News of the possible death of Abu-Khan's "son" was unsettling even though Jamal was in the pool a few feet away. She pulled him onto her lap for a moment, letting him drip all over her. He was with her and he was healthy and safe. But what about Rashid? Had he been in the old fortress when it was attacked? There was no reason for the news reports to mention *him*.

She didn't leave Mamad's house for two days after that. She sat in his living room next to the television, watching it and listening to the radio at the same time. Finally, on her fifth day in Tehran, she saw a broadcast of a speech made by Abu-Khan, who had been injured but was still very much alive. He looked smaller than she remembered. He looked tired, and he had a bandage on his forehead. His voice was choked and broken.

"Fellow countrymen, I have very sad news to impart to you today. My son, my beloved Jamal, was killed in the recent attack on the old fortress. My heart is broken. I have lost both his mother, my beautiful wife Karen, and now him, in the course of only a year. The one thing I have to live for now is my love for our great country."

Tears slid down his cheeks. He swiped at them with his linen handkerchief and then continued with patriotic rhetoric that Olivia barely heard. His supposed son was dead! He must have received her letter. He was surrendering Jamal to her!

Abu-Khan went on to announce that oil had been discovered in the eastern part of the country and a contract he'd signed with an American oil company would bring a great influx of wealth to Behruz. There would be a new prosperity. He outlined projects that were needed: running water for all citizens, better health care in the villages, more schools.

That part of his announcement could have been written by Rashid. Hopefully it *had* been. That would mean Rashid was alive when Abu-Khan was preparing the speech.

The next day, when there was still no word from Rashid, Mamad insisted they go to his villa on the Caspian Sea for a few days. He thought a change of scene would ease Olivia's stress. He would have his cell phone with him at all times, he assured her. Rashid would contact him as soon as he arrived in Iran.

But they didn't hear from Rashid, not the following day or the day after that. On the third day, Mamad went back to Tehran to check in at his office, Olivia walked on the beach after dinner while Soosi stayed in the villa with the children.

There were dozens of what the Iranians called "villas," which were like suburban homes in America, all in a row along the beach, all owned by wealthy Iranians from Tehran who used them for summer vacations and weekend getaways. It was a weekday, so few were occupied. Olivia had the beach to herself.

She carried her sandals and let her bare feet sink into the dark sand. The chador protected her from the cool sea breeze. After walking about half a mile, she stopped to sit on a concrete bench in front of one of the deserted villas, looking out over the soft swells of the sea. A dark ship loomed on the horizon, probably Russian.

She was exhausted from the effort of trying to keep her hopes alive. What would she do if Rashid never came? She would have to get on with her life for Jamal's sake. She would find a job. At least she would be able to lead a normal life, using her own name and raising her son openly. What a miracle it was that Jamal was thought to be dead. No one would have any reason to think he was not her child. Already, with his fair hair growing out and a healthy glow on his cheeks, he bore little resemblance to the sallow, black-haired boy Behruzis had seen posed stiffly in official government photos. She would have to change his name, and she would have to get him a birth certificate, but she would figure that out later.

To be able to live with her son without Abu-Khan's controlling presence was what she had dreamed of ever since she first held her baby in her arms, but it would be an empty life if Rashid didn't come back to share it.

She huddled bleakly into the cocoon of the chador, chilled by the breeze from the sea. The sun was about to set; it was time to go back.

She stood up. She looked back toward the villa, and there he was: a lone man walking toward her along the beach, a tall man wearing jeans and a blue T-shirt.

Rashid. Her heart sang his name; she wanted to run to him, but uncertainty overtook her. It was as it had been when she was younger. She would look forward to his visits with such longing, but then, when she actually saw him, she would freeze, not knowing what to say, not knowing how she was supposed to react. Not wanting to embarrass him by showing her feelings.

And so she stood there, watching him approach. He was alive. He'd come back to her.

He stopped a few feet away and gazed at her, his shoulders slumped in exhaustion. He needed a shave.

"Livie, I'm sorry about breaking my promise. Can you forgive me?"

"Oh, Rashid, I'm sorry about the things I said the night before you left. Can *you* forgive *me*?"

"Of course." He reached his hands up to grip the chador on either side of her face with fingers that trembled against her cheeks. He drew it away and arranged it around her shoulders like a shawl. Then he brushed his flat palms across her forehead, her temples, her jaw, her chin. Her lips. His eyes glistened with moisture.

"You had a right to be angry, Livie, and it was good that you expressed it. You were right. What happened wasn't your fault. I shouldn't have left. I should have tried harder to see you. I should never have trusted Abu-Khan. I let you down terribly, but I've paid for it. It was agony not seeing you and not knowing what went wrong. I've missed so much: I missed seeing you pregnant with my baby; I missed his birth and the early months of his life. I'm sorry I was angry when you told me, but it was such a shock. I know it wasn't your fault. I'm sorry for what you had to go through; I'm sorry I wasn't with you. I'll spend the rest of my life making it up to you if you'll let me."

"You don't have to do that, Rashid."

"God, Livie, I want to!" He gathered her against him resting his cheek against her hair. "You have to let me into your life; you have to stop fighting me. Can you do that?"

"Yes, Rashid." *Yes yes yes yes yes!*

He took a deep, sighing breath. Then he lifted her and spun her around, her hair flying behind her in the breeze.

"Tell me you love me," he demanded when he set her back on her feet. "I've waited too long to hear it."

Laughter bubbled from her. How could he place so much importance on the words? It seemed she had always loved him. She couldn't remember not loving him. Surely he had known.

"Say it, Livie."

"I love you, Rashid." She spoke slowly, enunciating carefully. She repeated it in Farsi. "*Doost set teram*."

"Thank God." His voice quaked. His grip tightened. He kissed her.

They sat together on the bench. "What are you looking forward to doing when you get back to the U.S.?" he asked.

"Everything! I want to shop in a mall and buy clothes for me and Jamal. I want to teach him to swim. I want to get him a sandbox. I want to drive—to be free to go wherever I want without having to arrange it with anyone. I want a piano. I want to dance. I want to go to a library. I want to eat pizza and tacos and potato chips and jellybeans and artichokes and…did I mention pizza? Especially pizza."

Rashid interrupted with his laughter. "I see you've given this some thought. I wish I'd known about the jellybeans. I could have brought you some."

She joined in his laughter. Joy and possibility fizzed through her veins.

"What else?" he asked. "Do you want to continue your music studies?"

"Not right now. I want to play, maybe in a community orchestra or something like that, but I don't want to go back to school, not yet anyway." She laughed a nervous laugh. "I want to focus on being a family for a while. I want to get married." Color rose to her cheeks. "To you. And I want more children."

Love and promises shone in his eyes. "I'm sure it can be arranged for all your wishes to come true."

"All of them?"

"Yes, darling Livie, most certainly all of them."

And then she remembered Abu-Khan. "What's happening in Behruz? Is Abu-Khan okay?"

"He's fine. His injury was slight. He made a speech."

"Yes, I heard it."

"Well, so did everyone in Behruz, and apparently they were all quite touched by his show of emotion and by his promise of prosperity. He appears to be gaining support."

"I could hardly believe he actually cried while he was making the speech. What a performance that was!"

"The tears were real, Livie. They were for you."

She gulped. She didn't want to hear that. "Well, if they were, it was because he couldn't stand to lose control over me; it wasn't because of love."

"Maybe. I'll admit Abu-Khan's idea of love is quite different from yours and mine. But I think he did actually feel remorse when he read your letter."

"Good. He should."

"Nur gave me some things for you." Rashid pulled a manila envelope from under his shirt and handed it to her.

Olivia tore open the envelope and took out two sheets of paper. The first one had her own signature at the bottom. It was the document she'd signed allowing Abu-Khan and Karen to adopt Jamal. The second paper was an official document with a baby's footprint at the bottom. "What?"

"It's a birth certificate for Jamal. It names you and me as parents."

"But where? How?"

"Apparently Karen gave both papers to Nur before she died. She told him he would know if the time ever came when you should have them."

He took the envelope and shook it upside down until something fell into his hand. It was an American passport. Her passport. A brash, happy eighteen-year-old version of herself smiled from the first page. Now the hope and confidence shining from that young face surged again.

"I hope Nur doesn't get in trouble for getting these things to me."

"Don't worry. Abu-Khan may never notice they're gone, and even if he does, I think Nur can hold his own with Abu-Khan." He pointed out that the space for the baby's name on the birth certificate had been left blank. "We can name him ourselves. We can give him an American name if you like."

"Yes. I would like that. Can we call him James after my father? Karen and I talked about naming him that when I was pregnant, but of course Abu-Khan had the final say."

Rashid agreed that James would be a fine name. They talked about how they would gradually introduce the change.

"We have all the time in the world," Rashid said.

All the time in the world. The promise of those words was as big as the Caspian Sea.

"It's about time we named the puppy too, don't you think?" Rashid asked.

Olivia laughed. "I've thought about that, but it

seems to be too late. I'm afraid he's just going to have to be known as *Puppy*."

"That name does have the advantage that Jamal already knows it."

"Exactly."

"I considered burning the adoption paper as soon as it was in my hands, but I thought you'd like to destroy it yourself."

"Oh yes! Can I do it right now?"

"I think right now is the perfect time."

She took the paper in trembling fingers and tore it lengthwise. She tore it again, crosswise, and then again and again until she had a pile of fragments in her hand. She stood up and took a few steps toward the foam of the receding waves. Rashid watched with approval beaming on his face. She spun around in the sand, her arms waving in a wide arc, her hand open, allowing the pieces of paper to be taken by the wind. Some went into the sea while others skittered across the sand. When she was done, she walked back to the bench, back to Rashid, back to the life that would be her future, joy vibrating through her veins. Rashid was back. He was safe. Jamal was theirs.

Rashid stood. He took her in his arms and kissed her again. He held her for a long time, pressing her head onto his shoulder and stroking her hair. "You're cold. Let's go back." He took her hand and led her toward the villa.

They stopped halfway, and Rashid took her other hand. "When can we be married?"

She let out a long blissful sigh. "Whenever you want. There's no hurry." *We have all the time in the world.*

"Good." He smiled a boyish grin she hadn't seen for a long time. "We'll get married in California if it's all right with you. My mother will help arrange it. She's going to love you, darling Livie, and she's going to be thrilled to have another grandchild." He kissed her again, a happy, celebrating, exultant kiss. Then he moved his lips to her ear and whispered, "I haven't been inside the villa yet. How big is it? Are we going to have a room to ourselves tonight?"

She laughed. "Yes. A room and a real bed."

"Good. I'll look forward to being alone with you later, because right now someone is about to join us."

Olivia turned her head toward the villa and saw Jamal toddling toward them. Mamad stood several yards behind him.

"Hello, son," Rashid said when Jamal reached them. He scooped up the boy and hugged him before settling him on his shoulder and then turning back to Olivia. "This boy's next word is going to be *Daddy*."

"Don't be so sure. I had in mind that it would be *Mommy*."

"Puppy!" Jamal cried gleefully. The puppy was racing toward them through the sand.

Olivia and Rashid laughed. Rashid put his free arm around Olivia's shoulders as they made their way back to the villa. The puppy trotted with them, making joyous leaps and circles at their feet.

A word about the author…

Judy was born in Kansas and raised in Minnesota. She now lives with her husband, Jim, in a small town in Oregon, where she works as a doula and childbirth educator. Her free time is devoted to grandmothering, gardening, embroidering, beachcombing, traveling, and, of course, writing.

www.ingramcontent.com/pod-product-compliance
Lightning Source LLC
Chambersburg PA
CBHW060931180626
46817CB00004B/1485